GUNS

"You let go of that woman," boomed the voice of the man staggering toward Slocum. "The god-damned slut."

Slocum gently nudged the woman away, stood up to face the belligerent stranger. Slocum saw that the man's face was puffy-red from anger or strong drink or both. He was trouble looking for some place to happen, and Slocum stood square in his path like a boulder on a narrow trail.

"Mister, you got your neck bowed and gravel-sand in your craw, but that don't give you the right to slander a fine woman."

"Who the hell you think you're talking to?" bellowed the red-faced man. "That's my daughter you're pawin' and slobberin' over, the little bitch."

Slocum saw red.

"Lovelace," said Slocum, "where I come from we don't talk about our women in saloons. And where I've been we don't slander a woman with foul language."

"You son of a bitch!" roared Jack Lovelace, and he waded into Slocum, both fists doubled-up like bludgeons and swinging...

OTHER BOOKS BY JAKE LOGAN

RIDE, SLOCUM, RIDE
SLOCUM'S CODE
SLOCUM'S FLAG
SLOCUM'S RAID
SLOCUM'S RUN
BLAZING GUNS
SLOCUM'S GAMBLE
SLOCUM'S DEBT
SLOCUM AND THE MAD MAJOR
THE NECKTIE PARTY
THE CANYON BUNCH
SWAMP FOXES
LAW COMES TO COLD RAIN
SLOCUM'S DRIVE
JACKSON HOLE TROUBLE
SILVER CITY SHOOTOUT
SLOCUM AND THE LAW
APACHE SUNRISE
SLOCUM'S JUSTICE
NEBRASKA BURNOUT
SLOCUM AND THE CATTLE QUEEN
SLOCUM'S WOMEN
SLOCUM'S COMMAND
SLOCUM GETS EVEN
SLOCUM AND THE LOST DUTCHMAN
   MINE
HIGH COUNTRY HOLDUP
GUNS OF SOUTH PASS
SLOCUM AND THE HATCHET MEN
BANDIT GOLD
SOUTH OF THE BORDER
DALLAS MADAM
TEXAS SHOWDOWN
SLOCUM IN DEADWOOD
SLOCUM'S WINNING HAND
SLOCUM AND THE GUN RUNNERS
SLOCUM'S PRIDE
SLOCUM'S CRIME
THE NEVADA SWINDLE
SLOCUM'S GOOD DEED
SLOCUM'S STAMPEDE
GUNPLAY AT HOBBS' HOLE

THE JOURNEY OF DEATH
SLOCUM AND THE AVENGING GUN
SLOCUM RIDES ALONE
THE SUNSHINE BASIN WAR
VIGILANTE JUSTICE
JAILBREAK MOON
SIX-GUN BRIDE
MESCALERO DAWN
DENVER GOLD
SLOCUM AND THE BOZEMAN TRAIL
SLOCUM AND THE HORSE THIEVES
SLOCUM AND THE NOOSE OF HELL
CHEYENNE BLOODBATH
SLOCUM AND THE SILVER RANCH
   FIGHT
THE BLACKMAIL EXPRESS
SLOCUM AND THE LONG WAGON TRAIN
SLOCUM AND THE DEADLY FEUD
RAWHIDE JUSTICE
SLOCUM AND THE INDIAN GHOST
SEVEN GRAVES TO LAREDO
SLOCUM AND THE ARIZONA COWBOYS
SIXGUN CEMETERY
SLOCUM'S DEADLY GAME
HIGH, WIDE, AND DEADLY
SLOCUM AND THE WILD STALLION
   CHASE
SLOCUM AND THE LAREDO
   SHOWDOWN
SLOCUM AND THE CLAIM JUMPERS
SLOCUM AND THE CHEROKEE
   MANHUNT
SIXGUNS AT SILVERADO
SLOCUM AND THE EL PASO BLOOD
   FEUD
SLOCUM AND THE BLOOD RAGE
SLOCUM AND THE CRACKER CREEK
   KILLERS
SLOCUM AND THE GUNFIGHTER'S
   GREED

JAKE LOGAN

SIXGUN LAW

BERKLEY BOOKS, NEW YORK

SIXGUN LAW

A Berkley Book/published by arrangement with
the author

PRINTING HISTORY
Berkley edition/May 1988

ISBN: 0-425-10850-3

A BERKLEY BOOK ® TM 757,375
Berkley Books are published by The Berkley Publishing Group
200 Madison Avenue, New York, N.Y. 10016.
The name "BERKLEY" and the "B" logo
are trademarks belonging to Berkley Publishing Corporation

PRINTED IN THE UNITED STATES OF AMERICA

10 9 8 7 6 5 4 3 2 1

1

John Slocum shook the brass-encased compass in his hand, watched the needle spin, dance, then come to a quivering halt. By his calculations, he was less than three miles from Fort Ellis. The fort was two and a half miles south of Bozeman. He had just crossed the foot of the mountain range a mile back, let the big rangy Missouri trotter blow for ten minutes before riding up to high ground. He clucked to the horse and was just about to rattle the reins and thump his spurs into the gelding's flanks when a moose broke from the trees and came to a startled halt some three hundred yards away.

Slocum sat stockstill in the Santa Fe saddle. The sorrel trotter, which he had been calling Stepper, stiffened and shot up its ears. The moose let out a bellow of surprise that sounded like a cross between the squeal of a pig and the bark of a wolf. Stepper nickered, and the moose lifted its head, swung its massive rack in Slocum's direction.

"Probably heading to the creek for water," said Slocum to himself, but there was no conviction in his tone. This was Crow country and he had been riding on pins and needles ever since he crossed the Yellowstone.

The moose turned at a right angle and broke into a shambling, awkward trot, away from the trail that led up to the creek. The creek, John knew, ran into the East Gallatin, and that was the way he had planned to ride into Bozeman City for supplies. The moose disappeared from sight and Slocum's green eyes narrowed to slits as he continued to gaze at the line of spruce that bordered the open meadow.

Stepper snorted and blew spray from his nostrils. Slocum swayed in the saddle as the horse bobbed its head and sniffed the light wind.

Something wasn't quite right, Slocum knew. The back of his neck bristled and his gut twisted as if someone had just put a knife to his spine.

"Stepper, what is it, boy?" Slocum asked, his voice a thin whisper.

The Crow burst from the line of spruce, galloped toward him. Slocum counted five braves before he rammed spurs into Stepper's flanks and yanked hard on the reins. The Crow braves yelped and slapped their wiry ponies into full gallop. Stepper's muscles bunched and the sorrel bolted into a run that ate up the yards. Behind him, Slocum heard the high-pitched yips of the Crow and the thunder of pony hooves pounding across the meadow.

The tall man flattened himself over the pommel, expecting an arrow or a rifle ball to streak toward him at any time. Stepper splashed across the meandering creek and plunged into a deep ravine. On his left, Slocum saw a perpendicular wall of limestone rock that rose a thousand feet above him. On his right, the mountain rose in steps or terraces, uneven in both height and distance, broken only by dense stands of spruce. In some places the dark green foliage jutted in a solid mass from base to summit; at others it was relieved by beetling cliffs of limestone weathered into fantastic shapes by the wind and rain of centuries.

The Crow raced after him, their blood-curdling cries bouncing off the limestone cliffs and fading into muffled echoes that were swallowed up in the staggered lines of trees on both sides of him. Slocum looked up and saw a huge rock that loomed from one of the highest points above the ravine. It looked strikingly like an old castle, its rampart and bulwark slowly yielding to the ravages of time. But the solid turret stood out in bold relief against the blue, cloudless sky with every embrasure chiseled to perfection, as though it had only been sculpted yesterday by the sure hand of man. It looked, Slocum thought, like the stronghold of some feudal baron, and he fully expected to see archers appear on the battlements, drawing their longbows to repel the invaders from below.

He rode for the summit, urging his mount through patches of timber. Antelope, foraging on the thick growth of bunch grass, leaped in front of him, scattered wildly, their tiny hoofbeats pounding on the earth as they streaked for cover. Slocum headed for the high ground, thinking he could put the "castle" between him and the Crow.

Topping the ridge, he reined Stepper over hard to his left through a heavy stand of spruce. When he broke out on the other side, he realized he had made a mistake. The bluffs rose up sheer in front of him. To his left, the escarpment dropped off. He rode to the right as hoofbeats thundered behind him and the Crows began yelping once again.

"They must know something I don't," Slocum said to the horse.

A hundred yards away, he saw that he had ridden into a box canyon. There was no way out unless he turned back.

If he did that, he'd run straight into the Crow. Stepper whickered and pranced around as Slocum tried to hold him from bolting back toward the direction from which they'd come.

"Shit," said Slocum. He considered leaving his horse and climbing up the rock walls, but he realized he wouldn't get very far. The only chance he had was to bluff his way through the Indians or just wait for them to enter the box and shoot down as many as he could before they overran him.

He rode back toward the entrance. When he emerged from the trees, the Crow were waiting for him. They surrounded him in an instant. One of them, a brave he took to be their leader, rode toward him cautiously.

"You give horse. Give guns," he said.

"Take 'em," said Slocum, forcing a grin.

The Crow grinned back. The others grunted and winded their ponies, riding them back and forth like strutting peacocks. Slocum swung out of the saddle. He unbuckled his gunbelt. Out of the corner of his eye, he looked them over. None of the Indians were painted for war. The leader was a handsome man, with shiny black hair, a straight nose that hooked slightly at the end, dark, wide-set eyes, sensuous lips. He looked to be no more than twenty-four or twenty-five. The others were about the same age. They appeared to be a hunting rather than a war party.

"Want boots," said the Crow leader. "You give pistol."

Slocum handed his gunbelt to the Crow. He sat down, pulled off his boots.

Another Crow rode up, pointed to Slocum's shirt. Slocum removed his shirt, handed it to him.

Still another wanted his trousers. Slocum stood there in his stockinged feet and long johns.

"Give hat," said another Crow. John sailed it to him and

the Crow laughed as he caught it deftly with one hand. He put it on his head.

"You have whiskey?" asked the leader.

"In my saddlebags," said Slocum. "Plenty whiskey."

"Good. You go quick, white man." The Crow made sign with his hands.

The Crow pointed toward the creek below them, to the south.

"Me name Big Wolf. You say white man's name."

"Slocum."

"Slow Come. Good. Slow Come go quick." He laughed, but there was no humor in it. Other Crow braves rode up, and they were leading two saddled horses. Shod horses. One of them held up a sack. "Plenty gold here," he said. "You got gold? You bad man?"

Slocum shook his head. He was puzzled by the Indian's reference to him being a bad man if he had gold on him. He started walking gingerly toward the creek. The Crow sat their horses and he had to walk among them. They scowled at him, and jeered when he stepped on a stone and did a one-legged dance.

"Fuck you," Slocum said under his breath. He crossed the creek, heard the Crow talking among themselves. He heard the creak of leather, turned to see one of them holding up the two whiskey bottles he kept in his saddlebags. Slocum smiled and dropped down over the ridge, out of sight. He began to run, zig-zagging along the creek until he came to a rolling plateau covered with prickly pear. He picked his way gingerly through the cactus.

He came to the river, swam it, emerged shivering on the other side. He looked back and saw no sign that the Indians had followed him. No, he thought, they'd be into the whiskey by now, and that was the beginning of their problems. He was about to seek shelter when he saw the trail, rutted with wagon tracks, leading through the trees that stippled a little knoll a few hundred yards away.

Elated, Slocum started out along the trail, hobbling along on tender feet. He entered the trees, covered another mile, dropped down into a clearing. Below, a valley sprawled for several miles. He saw buildings, smoke rising from chimneys as the sun began to drop toward the far peaks.

Funny, he had not known there was a town out here. This wasn't the Gallatin Valley, he knew that. He hadn't crossed the Beaverhead, so he must be near the Yellowstone, the river he had swum across. He began walking down the slope. Just outside the town he saw a small sign nailed to a stake that was driven into the ground. As he approached, he saw the name on the signboard: PIPESTONE.

"Never heard of it," he said to himself.

He walked into the town. Men looked at him strangely, then began to chuckle among themselves. Others laughed out loud. He looked closely at the men. Hardcases every one, unless he missed his guess.

The buildings were all new, built from whipsawed pine. There was something odd about the town. He saw no women, and the stores had no names on them, except for one. Someone had daubed paint on the false front of the biggest building in town. The lettering was crude, but the word was unmistakable. SALOON. Slocum headed for it on sore feet and men began to gather in groups and follow him.

"Where you goin', pilgrim?" asked one man.

"Anywhere I can sit down," replied Slocum.

More laughter.

"Bill, you better get your shovel and start diggin'," said a man standing in front of the saloon.

"Likely, we'll listen to his tune first," said Bill Hinson. "Man's got to have some story to tell."

The man who had spoken to Bill laughed sourly.

"Why he's jest pore folks come to call on us rich ones," said a man in the bunch behind Slocum.

"Don't say much, do he?" said another.

Slocum entered the saloon, squinted as he adjusted his eyes to the dimmer light. Several men stood at the long bar, others sat at tables. They all looked at him and at the bunch of men who crowded in behind Slocum. John looked at the walls, bare except for wanted posters tacked onto them here and there. There were no paintings or mounted game heads, just the wanted posters.

"Well, well, what have we got here?" said a man at the bar. "Some jaybird lookin' for a handout?"

"I'm not looking for a handout," said Slocum evenly, stepping toward the man. "I need the loan of a horse so I can get back my goods."

"Haw! Who got your goods, pilgrim? The bad men?"

"Crow name of Big Wolf, now that you ask," said Slocum.

A silence settled in the saloon. The man at the bar stepped up to Slocum, glared at him.

"You tryin' to be funny, mister?"

"Nothing funny about it. They chased me, ran me down and took my horse, my duds, everything I owned."

"You still got your hair, ain't ye?" said another man at the bar who stepped away from the rail.

"What's your name?" asked the man who stood in front of Slocum.

"John Slocum. You?"

"Rufus Harding. That there's Nate Bonstall at the bar. You come on over, have a drink with us. We want to parley about this Big Wolf son of a bitch."

"You know him?" asked Slocum.

"We'll ask the questions," said Harding. He was a raw-boned man, a foot shorter than Slocum, with a three-day beard on a lined face that only a mother could love. His rheumy blue eyes were set deep behind high cheekbones, straddled a flattened nose that bore the scars of a break or two. His lips were cracked from sun and wind and his hat sat atop a balding head. Nate Bonstall was leaner, taller, and more taciturn, with dark, wide-set eyes, a crooked smile, hawklike nose brooding over thin lips.

Both men looked over at a table in the center of the room. The man seated there, all alone, nodded quietly at Harding, as if giving his silent approval. Slocum followed Harding to the bar.

"Barry," said Rufus to the bartender, "you pour this man two fingers of Taos lightning." To Slocum he said, "If you survive it, I'll listen to your story, mister."

"And if we like your story, you'll get another," said Bonstall.

"And if you don't like my story?" asked Slocum.

"I'll kill you dead where you stand," said the humorless Nate Bonstall.

"You men are all heart," said Slocum.

"Mister, let me tell you something, and you listen real good," said Harding. "If you had come into Pipestone any other way than in your underwear, you'd be a dead man right now."

Slocum looked around at the faces of the others who had come into the saloon, and at the ones who had already been there. He found no sympathy, no friendliness. A cold chill rippled up his spine.

"I'll take that drink," he said quietly. "Seeing as it may be my last."

"You learn real quick, John Slocum," said Harding, as

Barry slid a glass of amber liquid toward him.

Slocum lifted the glass, turned it up as it reached his lips. The whiskey, tasting of hot pepper, tobacco, raw alcohol, and rattlesnake, burned his throat, hit his belly like molten lava. He felt the bile boil in his gut and start to rush up his throat, but he held it down. He forced a smile.

"Hell, that must be all of a day old," he said.

Harding laughed drily.

"Now you start talking, Slocum. I want to hear all about Big Wolf and them Crow braves you said stole your goods."

For emphasis, Harding pulled his Colt and cocked the hammer back. He aimed the pistol at Slocum's midsection and smiled crookedly.

Slocum swallowed. He didn't look at the pistol, but straight into Harding's eyes. He knew then that he was facing a killer who wouldn't hesitate to pull the trigger. And there wasn't a man there who would lift a finger to help him.

2

Slocum told his story of being run down by the Crow. He left nothing out, put nothing in that had not happened. He described the place where he had finally been caught and the listening men nodded. When he had finished, there was another stretch of silence that lasted for several seconds.

"Mister, your horse and gear are long gone," said Nate Bonstall, finally. "Them Crow are clear out of the country by now."

"No, I reckon not," said Slocum. "They were into the whiskey when I left. I figure they'll make camp right close to there. If I could borrow a horse, I'll find 'em by morning."

"Just like that, huh?" asked Harding. He eased the hammer back down on his Colt, shoved it back in its holster.

"You can ride along with me, if you want," said Slocum. "I'm not a horsethief."

"Haw, haw," laughed Harding. The others who had been

11

listening, joined in, began to laugh. "What do you think, Nate? Think we can trust this jasper?"

"'Bout as far as we can throw this here bar," said Bonstall.

"Let's you and me talk to Emmett over there for a dadgummed minute," said Harding. "Slocum, you just stay put and we'll see if we can't fix you up right quick."

Slocum stood there as Rufus and Nate walked over to the center table. He couldn't hear what they were saying, but the man they had called Emmett looked in his direction more than once. He wore a scowl on his face. Slocum couldn't detect his features very well. The brim of his Montana-creased hat shaded his face.

"Who're they talking to?" Slocum asked the bartender.

"Emmett Skaggs," said the barkeep. "He runs this town."

"I never heard of Pipestone before."

"Mister, you better start forgettin' you ever heard of it now."

Slocum thought about that, looked at the hardcases standing around him. Some of the faces matched those on the wanted posters. Had he stumbled onto an outlaw hideout? If so, it was pretty well kept up, and hidden. When he had tried to outrun the Crow, he had ridden well south of his ultimate destination. He had no real idea where he was, but he knew he was well off the main trails leading to the Gallatin Valley. Maybe west of the Yellowstone, east of the Beaverhead.

"How come you boys want to go after those Crow?" asked Skaggs.

"Well, we run into them ourselves early this morning," said Nate. "We didn't want to say much about it."

"They get anything?" asked Skaggs.

"Two thousand in gold," said Rufus wryly.

"You dumb sons of bitches," said Skaggs. He was a barrel-chested man, with a thick neck, slit eyes, a large bulbous nose, a shock of black hair. He had been a wrestler at one time, took to the owlhoot trail when he was fifteen, rustled cattle, robbed wagon trains. He was wanted for murder in half a dozen territories. He had been a guerrilla fighter during the War, but was essentially a man who liked to lead.

"We'd like to get our dust back," said Nate.

"I'm not sending any men with you," said Skaggs.

"We don't need any. We'll let this jasper track 'em, and get the jump on 'em. Them Crow wasn't wearin' paint."

"Be only three of you against half a dozen or so?"

"A dozen, maybe. We can take 'em," said Rufus confidently.

"If he don't do what you say," said Skaggs, "kill him."

"That would be my pleasure," said Rufus.

The two men walked away from Skaggs's table, back to the bar.

"You see any shod saddle horses with them Crow?" Rufus asked Slocum.

"Yeah. Two. Still had the saddles on. A sorrel gelding and chubby black mare."

"I'll buy you another drink, Slocum," said Nate. "Then we'll get some grub, put you down for the night. In the morning, we'll get some horses and track those Crow."

"I figure three hours ride," said Slocum.

"Well, we go after them before daylight."

"Those your horses I saw?" asked Slocum.

"Could be," said Nate. "We walked into town, same as you, only we got our clothes on."

"Yeah," said Rufus. "We jumped in the creek and let the

horses go when the Crow come after us. We shot at them and they skeedaddled out of there."

Nate poured a drink from his bottle into Slocum's glass. The whiskey was a little better than the tanglefoot. It warmed his insides without gagging him. Nate and Rufus had another drink. Rufus plunked coin on the bar and the three men left, headed for the hotel. The other men remained in the bar and the main street was almost deserted. Harding and Bonstall flanked Slocum and he knew that he was virtually a prisoner.

They headed for the hotel at the end of the street. They passed another saloon, this a log cabin with a sod roof that had a name, OWLHOOT, and Slocum heard voices and laughter inside. He heard a woman laugh and his eyebrows arched in surprise.

"You can grub with us at the Pinetree Lodge," said Rufus, "and bunk with Bonstall. Any objections?"

"Nope," said Slocum.

The Pinetree Lodge had a dining room and bar. Slocum and the two men ate beefsteak and potatoes, washed it down with hot coffee.

"You'll pay us when you get your goods back," said Bonstall, picking his teeth with the point of his knife when they were finished eating.

"Be glad to," said Slocum.

He slept that night on a rug in Bonstall's room, listened to the man snore most of the night. When he awoke in the morning, he was stiff, but the soreness had gone out of his feet. He stretched, woke up Bonstall. They met Harding in the restaurant, filled up with flapjacks and beef cut into thin strips. Harding took a sack of cooked beef with him to eat on the trail.

They headed for the stables as the sun began to rise in the morning sky. The day promised to be warm. Slocum was glad. He was shivering in his union suit.

They saddled three horses, led them out onto the street.

"You make a break for it," Harding told Slocum, "and we'll both fill you full of lead."

"Let's get to it," said Slocum, climbing into the saddle. They had given him a blue roan, a gelding, that seemed fitted for the mountains. It was sure-footed, quick to respond to the reins. He felt odd riding in his underwear and bootless, but it couldn't be helped.

"Lead out," said Bonstall, and Slocum headed for the track he had followed in to the town. He was still puzzled over Pipestone, its denizens. He hadn't figured it all out yet, but he had a pretty good idea that the men who lived there were all outlaws. How they made a living, he didn't know, but there was plenty of opportunity for brigands bent on making a dishonest living in Montana Territory.

The threesome picked their way up the slope, away from the town. When Slocum looked back, he saw that Pipestone had disappeared in the jagged rows of trees that stippled the hillside. It was a perfect hideout, he thought, very defensible.

Three hours later, they came to the place where the Crow had cornered Slocum. His green eyes burned when he recalled how he had been overtaken and robbed by Big Wolf and his band.

"This the place?" asked Harding, looking at the roil of tracks.

"Yeah," said Slocum.

"What now?" asked Bonstall.

"I figure we'll find them in an hour or so. They won't go far."

"You seem pretty sure about that," said Nate.

"I'm pretty sure," said Slocum enigmatically. He looked

at the soft tracks in the dirt. He began to follow them, his
two captors just behind him, on either flank.

The trail led away from the rocky peak, through the
spruce, easterly along the creek. The Crow tracks narrowed to single file and once, Slocum saw where they had
stopped, their horses in a circle. He smiled.

"Won't be long now," he said.

"You are mighty free with your predictions," said Nate
sarcastically. "Looks like they had a pow-wow here."

"Maybe stopped to take a few swigs of whiskey," said
Slocum.

"You can tell that by the tracks? Bullshit."

"They didn't roll smokes," said Slocum.

He continued on, alert to any sound or movement. The
dew had burned off the tracks, and they were plain to read
as he threaded his way through the timber. A half hour
later, they came to a meadow, heard the whicker of horses
beyond the fringe of trees at the border.

Slocum reined up the roan, looked at the two men behind him.

"Just ahead, I'd say."

"I heard the horses," said Nate, drawing his pistol.
Rufus slipped his rifle from its scabbard, levered a shell
into the chamber of the .44-40 Henry.

"You go on ahead, Slocum," said Harding. "One bad
move and you'll get a lead slug in your back for sure."

Slocum's eyes narrowed, but he said nothing. He rode
out from the trees, saw the horses beyond a jumble of
rocks. A stream meandered through the meadow. Butter-
flies danced over the grasses and insects droned. The sun
was climbing toward its noon zenith and a soft breeze blew
across the open spaces.

He rounded the rocks, saw the Crows there, sprawled as
if they were drunk, or asleep. The hobbled ponies and

horses whickered at him as he rode up. He stopped, turned and gestured to the two outlaws. Moments later, Harding and Bonstall rode up, their guns at the ready.

"Jesus Christ," said Bonstall, when he saw the Indians. "Out cold."

"Dead, more likely," said Slocum.

"Dead?" asked Harding. "How?"

Slocum swung out of the saddle. He walked over to Big Wolf, picked up the almost empty whiskey bottle lying alongside. The Crow were all dead, he knew. Their bodies had not yet started to bloat because they lay in the shade of the rocks, but the smell of death lingered in the air. The other two men dismounted. Slocum gave the bottle to Harding.

"Don't drink it," he said. "Just smell it."

Harding sniffed the opening, jerked his head back.

"Whiskey. What else?"

"Strychnine," said Slocum.

"Christ," said Harding. "They're all dead, aren't they?"

Slocum looked around. Some of the Indians had crawled to the creek. One of them lay facedown in the water. Another was doubled up, as if he had died in agony. Still another lay draped over a log, his face contorted, black from suffocation.

Bonstall gagged, fought to keep the bile from rising in his throat.

"Christ," Harding said again.

Slocum started counting the bodies. Something was wrong, but he couldn't put his finger on it. A moment later, as he walked between Harding and the pile of rocks, he knew what was amiss. One of the Crow he had seen the day before was missing.

Slocum looked up, then, saw the shadow appear atop the pile of rocks.

The Crow brave, a knife in his hand, leaped straight for Harding, whose back was turned.

"Look out!" cried Slocum, and threw himself at the plunging Crow. His shoulder struck the brave in the hips, twisted him away from his course of flight. Slocum pitched headlong into the dirt. The fall knocked the air from his lungs. The Crow scrambled to his feet, dove at Slocum, his knife poised to plunge into Slocum's chest.

Slocum rolled, and kicked a stockinged foot into the Indian's groin. The Crow grunted and tumbled next to Slocum. Slocum regained his footing. The Crow crouched and charged straight at the tall white man, his face a mask of determination.

"Kill him!" yelled Harding.

"Arrgh!" croaked Bonstall, still sick from seeing the dead Indians.

Slocum brought down a hammering fist and smashed the Crow square in the back. But the Indian didn't go down. Instead, he twisted deftly away and brought his knife up high over his head. He plunged it downward. Slocum's right hand shot out. He grasped the Crow brave's wrist, and the two locked together, wrestled for possession of the gleaming weapon. Back and forth they danced. Cords stood out in the Indian's arms and back as he tried to wrestle Slocum to the ground. Slocum's powerful legs pumped, drove the Indian backwards until the brave side-stepped. Still, Slocum held onto the red man's wrist, even as he whirled around, fought to maintain his balance.

"You die, white man," growled the brave.

Slocum grabbed the Indian's wrist with his other hand. The two men fell to the ground as Slocum kicked one leg out from under the warrior. They rolled in the grass. Bonstall and Harding tried to get a shot. Bonstall started to fire his pistol, but Harding restrained him.

"You might kill Slocum," he said.

"Kill 'em both, who gives a damn," snarled Bonstall.

"You just hold on, Nate," warned Rufus.

Slocum felt the Indian's strength in his arm and wrist. The knife crept closer to his throat as his own grip weakened. He flipped onto his back, felt the brave's hot breath on his face. The knife blade drew still closer to his Adam's apple. The Indian's black eyes glittered like sunstruck agates.

"The Crow's got him," said Bonstall, licking dry lips.

"Shut up, Nate," husked Harding.

Slocum summoned up all his strength and wrenched the Indian's wrist sideways. The Indian lost his grip on the knife. He lunged for it as it fell toward Slocum, grasped at it. But Slocum was quicker. He lashed out, grabbed the knife by its thong-wrapped handle, and rolled over onto the Crow's waist, pinning him to the ground.

The Crow brought a knee up into Slocum's groin. The knee sank in and pain shot through Slocum's loins. A wave of nausea enveloped Slocum. The pain made him dizzy. The Crow beneath him swam in and out of his blurred vision.

Pressing his advantage, the brave kicked upward, squirmed out from under Slocum's weight. The Crow wrapped an arm around Slocum's neck, began to squeeze. Slocum felt the pressure on his windpipe, then his air shut off. He struggled to breathe, fought off the blackness that rolled in on him.

The Crow squeezed harder and Slocum felt himself sinking down into a pit, down into the black void of death. He heard the grunt of victory in his ear, felt the hot breath of the Indian against his face as he crumpled, suddenly drained of all strength.

"You die, white eyes," rasped the Crow in English.

And Slocum knew he had only seconds of life left to him. Death was dancing just beyond his blurred vision, waiting to shroud him in its eternal cloak of darkness.

3

Slocum made his whole body go limp. The Crow's sweat-slick arms relaxed for just the smallest part of a second and Slocum twisted his neck, slipped his chin downward to break the Indian's grip on his throat. Still gripping the knife, he drove it backward into the Crow's side, felt the blade sink through flesh. His hand turned sticky from the gush of blood that drenched his knuckles.

The brave cried out in pain, and Slocum drew in a lungful of precious air. He slithered free of the Indian's grasp and turned, drawing the bloody knife backwards for another thrust. Savagely, he drove the blade into the Crow's belly, slashed sideways, cut through the abdomen and wrenched the blade back through the flesh.

The brave doubled over; his intestines spilled from his rent stomach. The Crow grabbed his belly. His hands filled with blood. The brave quivered and collapsed, mortally wounded, onto the grass. Slocum stood up, panting, swayed over the dying Indian for a moment, then drove the blade downward, sank it into the Indian's back. His blood-slickened hands released their grip on the handle and Slocum staggered backward, his burning lungs sucking in soothing oxygen, his blurred vision settling into focus.

"Christ," said Harding, "you done him good, Slocum."

The Crow kicked once and then was still. One of his fingers twitched for several seconds, then stopped.

"Ooeee, I never seen nothin' like that," breathed Bonstall. "I thought you was a goner for sure, Slocum. Your face was turnin' purple as a boiled beet."

"Better start looking for your gold," said Slocum. "I'm going to get my clothes on and saddle up."

Slocum wiped his bloody hand on his long johns, walked over to the pile of goods, found his clothing. He dressed, found his boots, pulled those on. His pistol, saddle, and rifle lay in a heap next to a dead Crow. He strapped on his gunbelt.

Bonstall let out a whoop, held up the sack of gold. He and Harding did a little jig while Slocum saddled Stepper. Slocum checked his saddlebags, saw that his rifle was loaded. He looked once again at the dead Indians.

"Pretty good trick," said Harding.

"A little insurance I carry in Crow country," said Slocum. "Whiskey and strychnine. Trick I learned from a mountain man down in Virginia City."

"Mister, me and Nate want to show our appreciation. Here's a hundred dollars, fifty from each of us. You saved us about two thousand in gold."

Rufus handed Slocum the money. Bonstall grinned wide. "You come on back to Pipestone with us and your pockets won't be empty," said Harding.

"Plenty of women and no law," said Bonstall.

Slocum considered it. There was something about Pipe-

stone that bothered him. Not only had he never heard of
the town, but he was sure that every man there was wanted
by the law. But, there were many such places in the West:
border towns, outlaw camps, hidden valleys. There was
something different about Pipestone, though. It was well-
built and no one seemed worried about the law. Why? Slocum wondered. Who ran the town? How did the outlaws
make their money?

Slocum was not an outlaw, but he rode in places where
there was no law. Ever since the War, he had been a home-
less man, one of those southerners who went back only to
find that the carpetbaggers had moved in, the judges had
filled their pockets, the land grabbers had taken over good
bottom land for taxes. Calhoun County, Georgia was typi-
cal of those places that had been ravaged and pillaged by
men who had never carried a gun, by men who had never
fought a battle or a war. Bitterly, Slocum had vowed never
to go back home. There was nothing there for him anymore. Out West, a man could be free. He could use any
name he wanted and no one asked him where he was from
or where he was going.

"Well, Slocum, how about it?" asked Harding. "You
want to throw in with us? We ride for Emmett Skaggs and
he's the best there is. He's canny as a fox, that one, and me
and Nate think you and him'd get along just fine."

"Skaggs? Don't know the man."

"I've rid a river or two with him," said Harding.

"Come on, Slocum, make up your damned mind. This
place plumb gives me the willies," said Bonstall.

Slocum shrugged.

"Hell, I ain't doin' nothin' anyways," he drawled. "I'll
ride back to Pipestone with you, look things over. If I get a
good enough offer, I'll stay."

Harding and Bonstall let out a spontaneous cheer. Harding slapped Slocum on the back.

"Come on, then, let's ride," said Rufus. "We got what we came for. Let the buzzards have these damned thievin' Crow."

Bonstall forced a grin. He did not look back at the bodies of the dead Indians. Already they were beginning to ripen in the sun. Jays squawked in the trees and a pair of prairie swifts slashed by overhead. Harding led out, and Slocum rode in the middle, Bonstall at the rear. He may have been an invited guest, but his hosts were still acting more like guards than friendly companions. Slocum kept an eye on Bonstall, just in case.

He sure as hell didn't want to get a bullet in the back.

Slocum put up at the Pinetree Lodge, a clapboard hotel that charged six bits a night. He had money besides the hundred dollars Harding and Bonstall had given him. He had promised to meet the pair at the Owlhoot Saloon, the soddy he had seen earlier, that evening. That afternoon he slept and his dreams were full of faceless men and giant Indians that rode out of the darkness on skeletal ponies that sounded like thunder.

But the thunder woke him up and he realized that someone was pounding on his door. He rubbed the sleep out of his eyes, reached for his gunbelt that was hanging on the bedpost. He strapped it on, stalked across the floor.

"Who is it?" he rasped.

"A friend," said a man's voice on the other side of the door.

Slocum opened the door a crack, peered through the opening. He saw a scraggly-bearded man with a crumpled hat, pimpled nose, and a toothless mouth looking up at him with rheumy, red-rimmed eyes that swam like marbles in a bottle of oil.

"Yeah?" said Slocum.

"Stranger, let me in quick. I got somethin' to jaw with you about."

Slocum opened the door. The old man waddled in, looked all around the room, plunked himself down in a straight-backed chair. There were only two in the room, and they braced either side of a table that was scarred with knife marks and cigarette burns.

"What's on your mind?" asked Slocum.

"The name's Freddie Willits and I've heard some about you. It's all over town how you buffaloed them Crow with pizened whiskey. Harding's callin' you some kind of hero."

"Harding's a damned fool."

Willits cackled and slapped a knee with the flat of his palm.

"Mister, you ain't as dumb as I look. I'm just surprised you rode back with those two. Man as smart as you would've been twenty mile from here by now, I'd reckon."

"Maybe I wanted to ride back with them."

"You ain't the law, are ye?"

"Willits, you ask too many damned questions."

"Just tryin' to get the drift of the wind, Slocum."

"Well, you got a big nose."

"Haw, I do, yair, I shore do. But I seen you come in yestiddy, and I knew a man had walked into Pipestone. If you hadn't been damned near nekkid as a jaybird, you wouldn't have lasted five minutes."

"What do you mean?" asked Slocum.

"I mean, Slocum, that nobody gets in and nobody gets out lessen Emmett Skaggs says so."

"Where do you fit in?"

"I run freight for Skaggs," said Willits. "Haul in supplies for the town, pick up information."

"What kind of information?"

"Wagon trains, money shipments, cattle drives."

"So that Skaggs can rob them." It was a flat statement. Slocum's eyes narrowed. Skaggs seemed to be pretty well organized and there were enough outlaws in town to make up a small army. The more he learned about Pipestone, the less he liked about it.

"Sure. They ain't a minute goes by that Emmett he don't have scouts out, too. They comes and they goes all day long. When they's somethin' big cookin' in the pot, Skaggs and his bunch goes out and comes back with money and blood on their hands."

"Why are you telling me all this, Willits?"

"You reminded me of somebody I knew once't, maybe."

"Who's that?"

"My own son."

"What happened?" asked Slocum.

"Dunno. But Emmett says he'll be comin' back one day, so I wait here and do work for Skaggs, hopin' he'll ride in."

"But you don't think so."

Willits shook his head, worked his lips over toothless gums. Slocum felt sorry for the old man. In his gnarled hands with the cracked flesh at the knuckles, he saw the years of pain and hardship, the sear of wind and weather, the broken dreams of another man who had come West to find his fortune and discovered only the hardness of living in a harsh land full of hidden dangers.

"Jackie was a good boy, a little wild at times, but not bad-hearted like some. He come out here with me from Mississippi and he got in with some of the rowdies in Virginia City. We was havin' hard times and he took up with Skaggs's bunch. Skaggs never let on what it was he did or what he had in mind, but some time ago, Emmett he got the idee of buildin' hisself a town out here. He wanted it to look like a town, but be like a fort—a hideout. And, that's what he done. Jackie he didn't like it none when Skaggs took to killin' and I think he wanted to ride out."

"But you think Skaggs wouldn't let him go," said Slocum.

"Mister, we're all prisoners here in Pipestone. One way er t'other. I figger ever' damn man and woman here owes a soul to Emmett Skaggs. He's a devil." The last was delivered in a whisper and the words sent a shiver up Slocum's spine.

"You got any proof?"

"Don't need none. You'll find out for yourself. Jest try and ride out of Pipestone now that you know where it is. Either you'll get a lead slug in the back, or you'll run into more guns than you can shake a stick at."

"Harding and Bonstall invited me back here. I could have ridden on my way after I got my horse back."

Willits looked at Slocum as if an idiot had just spoken.

"You think so? I'll bet nickels to double eagles that Emmett told them to kill you unless you come back with 'em."

Slocum wondered. At the time he hadn't thought much of it, but he had that feeling, still, that he had been a prisoner ever since he rode out with Bonstall and Harding. Even on the way back, one or the other of them was always close by, watching him.

"That may be."

"Why did you come back, Slocum? You ridin' the owl-hoot trail?"

"No, I don't reckon. Curious, I guess."

"I don't buy hogwash."

"Something Harding said about Pipestone. He said there was no law here. Maybe I wanted to see if it would work."

"Oh, there's law here, Mr. John Slocum. Emmett Skaggs is the law. He don't call it that, but he runs things with a mean eye and an iron hand. You'll see."

"How come you're telling me all this? Maybe you guessed wrong about me. If I was to tell Skaggs what you said, he might put your lamp out."

"I read men pretty good. You won't tell him, because there'll come a day when you'll go up against him, gun to gun. I've seen your kind before. You don't have no home, and people think you're a saddle tramp. You keep to your own self and you don't like people crowding you. Man like you comes along, I figger you're gonna be a burr under somebody's saddle pretty quick."

"I've seen bad law in some places," said Slocum, with a trace of bitterness.

"Me too, I reckon. But you got backbone. Not like Skaggs. He's a skulker, that one. He's a night rider for sure. You'll go up agin' him, and I just wanted you to know here's one who will back you."

"What about your son?"

"I don't reckon he'll ever be back. I give up on him a long time ago."

"But you don't know for sure."

"No," said Willits, shaking his head sadly. "That's why I keep on runnin' supplies for Skaggs and his bunch. I keep hopin' Jack's alive and he'll come back to get me."

"Well, maybe he will." But Slocum didn't believe it. He didn't fully trust Willits, but he was grateful to the man for coming forward and speaking out. He wondered how a man like Skaggs could have such a powerful hold on so many people. There were men like that, he knew, but they were usually politicians. Maybe it was the money. Maybe that was what gave Skaggs his power. Ill-gotten or not, some men would kill their own mothers for money. Maybe Skaggs was like a magnet and he attracted such men.

"Don't sit with your back to no doors," said Willits, rising from his chair. "And if you tell Skaggs I come here, I'll call you a baldfaced liar."

"Don't worry," said Slocum. "But I don't know what you expect of me. I'm a stranger here."

"Ride with Skaggs. See what he does. They's a lot of people here would like to get out. Maybe you're the man to lead us out of the Valley of Death."

"I doubt it," said Slocum. "But who else has Skaggs got under his boot?"

"You might meet up with a young filly name of Melanie Lovelace. She's one. Now, I got to git. I got mules to groom. Headin' out for supplies tomorry first light. You watch your back, Slocum."

"You take care, Willits."

The old man left the room and Slocum shut the door after him. He stood there for a long time as the sun set and the shadows filled up the room.

Now, more than ever, Slocum wanted to find out all he could about Pipestone and the hardcases who worked for Emmett Skaggs.

He had the odd feeling that he was in the wrong place at the wrong time. But something held him there, something pulled at him to stay.

Maybe he was the one to go up against Emmett Skaggs.

Toe to toe. Gun to gun.

4

The Owlhoot Saloon was bigger inside than it looked from the outside. It had a long bar and tables and chairs. There were no wanted posters stuck to the walls, but they had put a Mexican serape on one wall, hung some gourds, spurs, cinch rings and such on the others just to break up the monotony of the chinked logs. Lanterns hung from the beams that held up the sod roof. When Slocum walked in, men were playing dominoes and cards, drinking whiskey and warm beer, talking in low tones as if expecting him.

Rufus Harding stepped away from the bar, beckoned for Slocum to come over. Nate Bonstall, his back to the front door, turned and looked at Slocum, smiled. Slocum strode across the dirt floor of the saloon, his senses alert. He had the feeling he was being tested, put on display by these two.

"Have a drink, Slocum. You earned it," said Harding. "Boys, this here's John Slocum, what sent them thievin'

31

Crow to the happy hunting grounds and never batted an eye."

Some of the patrons cheered and applauded mildly. Slocum half-bowed, took a place at the bar.

"Name your poison," said Bonstall.

"The whiskey any worse here than in the other place?"

"Haw," guffawed Harding. "Kelly, put out a bottle of your best whiskey for Slocum. Old Overholt suit you?"

"I've tasted worse."

"You've got wit, Slocum. I told Emmett what you done and he's mighty impressed."

"I'd like to meet him," said Slocum.

"Well, you will, but not right away. Me 'n' Nate got to see him later on business."

"That why you wanted to meet me here?" asked Slocum.

"Partly. The Pipestone Saloon, that's what we call it anyways, is kind of Emmett's own private place. Hell, a few months ago, this town was mostly tents. Now we got real buildings. Our own town."

The bartender set a bottle of Old Overholt on the bar, a thick shotglass alongside it. Slocum pulled the cork, poured himself three fingers. The whiskey went down smooth.

"You just have yourself a high time here tonight and we'll see you in a few days," continued Harding. "Emmett, he don't make friends real easy."

"You going somewhere?" asked Slocum.

"Maybe," said Harding, evasively. "Like I said, we got business with Skaggs. There'll be some music here by and by, and some pretty girls to take your mind off your troubles."

"I might ride on tomorrow," said Slocum.

"Well, now, what's your hurry?" asked Bonstall. "Hell, you just got here."

"Better stick around," said Harding quickly. "When we get back, we may have a proposition for you."

"How long will you be gone?"

"Few days," said Harding.

"Long time to sit and do nothing."

"Yeah, well, take my advice and wait for us."

Slocum didn't think they could put it any plainer. As Willits had said, he was virtually a prisoner in Pipestone. He had a feeling that someone would be dogging his footsteps every place he went. As a matter of fact, he'd had the feeling that someone was following him when he walked down the street to the Owlhoot Saloon. He didn't see anyone, it was just a feeling. But, a strong feeling at that.

"I'll wait for you," said Slocum.

"Good, good," said Harding, his mouth stretching in a wide grin.

Bonstall said nothing, but there was a smug look on his face that looked as if it had been starched and ironed on hot.

Harding and Bonstall finished their drinks. Harding threw a bunch of tokens on the bartop and slapped Slocum on the back.

"You have yourself some fun," he said.

"Be seein' ya," said Bonstall, and there was a warning in his eyes as he followed Harding out of the saloon. Slocum picked up one of the tokens and examined it. It was made of brass, stamped on both sides. One side read "Pipestone—Legal Tender, One Dollar." On the other was a likeness of a man with a bandana over his face.

Skaggs's little joke, thought Slocum. He tossed the brass token back into the pile. Kelly, the bartender, gathered them up, put them in a cigar box on the back bar. He was a rotund man with an unlit cigar stuck in his mouth, a soiled apron around his middle. He had hairy arms and thick wrists that jutted out of a chambray shirt. His nose was squashed like a mushroom. His whole face was a mass of lumps. He looked like a pugilist, thought Slocum.

"What's there to do in town besides drink?" Slocum asked him.

"You can play cards or checkers, dominoes. Some of the gals will be in later. They charge a buckskin apiece. You got tokens, same as cash."

"I'll take me a table," said Slocum, fisting the bottle at the neck. He walked to a table in the far corner, sat down. He was glad he had eaten before coming to the saloon. He felt good after the hot bath, too. He had shaved and he felt almost human after being on the trail for the past two weeks. He could take Pipestone for a few days. He wondered, though, how long he could remain neutral. He would be interested to see what Harding and Bonstall would have to say to him after returning from their trip.

He looked around the room at the few men who sat at tables playing cards, checkers, or dominoes. They didn't look like hardcases. None of them seemed to be carrying weapons, at least not in the open. They seemed to be ordinary men relaxing after a hard day's work.

Money, he thought. Some men would do anything for it, no questions asked. He wondered if the men in the saloon were not captives like himself, for one reason or another. Here were the blacksmiths, the wheelwrights, the shopkeepers, the stablemen. Money drew them to Pipestone and once they were in Skaggs's town, they were under his control. Perhaps some of them, realizing where the money came from, wanted to get out. But, according to Willits, they were not allowed to leave Pipestone.

The girls began arriving around nine that evening. They

were painted and powdered, wore short skirts and mesh stockings. Most of them sat with men they knew. One went to the bar and Kelly gave her a tray and a clean towel, a clay bowl full of change. She was fair of face, young, and wore little makeup, unlike the glitter gals who sat on the men's laps. The piano man came out and started banging out "Sweet Betsy from Pike," and he was soon joined by a banjo player and a man carrying a big bass.

Slocum sipped his drink slowly.

The girl at the bar went around to the various tables and took drink orders. She emptied ashtrays and brought fresh cigars to those who ordered them. The hem of her dress fell just below her knees, and Slocum could see that she had trim ankles. Her calico dress snugged against pert breasts and she wore a cameo pendant suspended around her neck on a velvet ribbon.

The piano man banged out "Green Grow The Lilacs," and the girl came over to Slocum's table.

"If this were 'Lady's Choice,'" she said softly, "I'd pick you."

"Huh?" said Slocum.

"I've been watching you out of the corner of my eye. You're new here."

"I am."

"Are you the one they're all talking about?"

"I wouldn't know."

"You're not one of Skaggs's boys."

"No."

"I'm Melanie. What's your name?"

"Slocum."

"That's all? Just Slocum."

"John."

She laughed then, and her bright laugh rose above the music and her smile was dazzling white, like sunstruck snow on a mountain peak. Slocum thought then how different she was from the usual saloon gal he had met in cowtowns and trail camps since the War. Melanie didn't seem to be the kind of lusty woman with a name like Hambone Jane or Squirrel-tooth Alice. There was something refined about the way she moved and spoke. Something genteel in her manner, as though she had been raised well, not chased into the corn crib by her older brother or her uncle or bedded in the hayloft by every gap-toothed sodbuster kid who came by the farm selling black apples and sour milk for the hogs.

"Can I bring you something?" she asked.

"Not unless it's information," he replied.

Melanie cocked her head, squinted suspiciously with one eye.

"What do you mean?"

"I'd like to know where Skaggs gets all his power. Why this town is here. A whole lot of things."

"Mister, people who ask questions like that don't live very long. Not in Pipestone."

"So, you're one his bunch too?"

"Whose bunch?"

"Skaggs's. He's the ramrod here, isn't he?"

"Slocum," she said, "I don't know who you are or where you came from, but I'm not in anybody's bunch."

"You work here. You work for Skaggs."

Her complexion flushed to a rosy pink. Her eyes flashed fire. For a moment, Slocum thought she was going to whack him alongside of the head with her tray. Instead, she leaned over the table, glared at him, eye to eye from a scant six inches. He could see the mounds of her breasts pushing out of her bodice, creamy soft, inviting.

"I work here because my father works for Skaggs. My mother's dead, my pa's an outlaw. But I hate this life. I hate Emmett Skaggs. And, I think I hate you, too."

"I'm sorry to hear that," Slocum said drily.

She backed off, then, but the glare was still there, the frost and fire in her eyes. He couldn't keep his mind off those breasts of hers. He had been a long time without a woman, and it had been longer still since he had seen one so fair.

"Maybe you'd better mind your own business," she said. "And, speaking of that, if you don't work for Skaggs, just what are you doing in Pipestone?"

"Damned if I know. I came here by mistake, and now it looks like I can't leave."

Her look softened. Her mouth began to quiver as if she was going to say something, but she pursed her lips and spun away from him.

"Wait," said Slocum, not loudly, but urgently.

She turned, stared at him with a puzzled expression on her face.

"Maybe I can help," he said simply, low enough so that the others in the room could not hear.

She walked slowly back towards him and he saw that she had uncommon grace and poise. This was no tramp, but a woman in possession of herself. Still, he wondered about her. Willits had mentioned her name.

"How?" she asked.

"Willits said you might want to talk to me."

"Did he say that?"

"Not in so many words. But he said there are some who would like to get out of this valley."

"So?"

"So, maybe I could help," said Slocum.

She came closer, looked over her shoulder to see if she was being watched. Then she fixed her eyes on Slocum's and bent her neck slightly.

"If my pa or Skaggs even knew I was talking to you about such a thing, I'd get skinned alive and you'd be getting measured for a pine box. You mustn't say these things."

"I want to help," he said lamely.

"Not here. Not now. And I'm not sure I can trust you."

"You can. If you want to, Melanie."

"You don't understand. My father, he—"

She stopped, looked toward the door. A man stood there, swaying slightly. The man was stocky, muscular, had his hat on crooked as if he had dressed in the dark. His face was etched with deep lines around the mouth and in the forehead. Hooked nose, dark blue eyes, thin lips. He blinked, looked around the room. He saw Melanie and lurched toward her.

Melanie uttered a weak cry and suddenly threw her arms around Slocum. He slammed back in his chair, encircled her instinctively with his own arms to keep from being bowled over.

"Don't let him touch me," she whispered. Slocum's nostrils filled with the faint and tantalizing tang of her perfume. Her hair pressed against his face, soft and silky, smelling fresh as rain.

"You let go of that woman," boomed the voice of the man staggering toward Slocum. "The goddamned slut."

Slocum gently nudged the woman away, stood up to face the belligerent stranger. Slocum saw that the man's face was puffy-red from anger or strong drink or both. He was trouble looking for someplace to happen, and Slocum stood square in his path like a boulder on a narrow trail.

"Mister, you got your neck bowed and gravel-sand in your craw, but that don't give you the right to slander a right fine woman." Slocum's voice boomed in the saloon and every man and woman there heard him clear and plain.

"Who the hell you think you're talking to?" bellowed the red-faced man. "That's my daughter you're pawin' and slobberin' over, the little bitch."

Slocum saw red.

"Lovelace," said Slocum, "where I come from we don't talk about our women in saloons. And where I've been we don't slander a woman with foul language."

"You son of a bitch!" roared Jack Lovelace, and he waded into Slocum, fists doubled-up like bludgeons and swinging. Slocum, caught by surprise, felt a fist rocket into his jaw and another slam into his midsection with the force of a pile-driver. He staggered backwards, star clusters exploding in his brain, salty tears stinging his eyes.

Lovelace pressed his advantage, bulling forward, shoulder down, fists and arms working like pistons. Slocum danced away, his boots scuffing up the dirt as he balled his fists, dropped into a fighting crouch. Lovelace whirled, teetered for a moment, threw another punch. Slocum caught the blow on his shoulder, flicked a left hook to Lovelace's jaw, followed up with a straight right to the chest.

Lovelace, though drunk, was solid bone and gristle. Slocum felt his fists crunch flesh and Lovelace rolled with both punches, absorbed them and scooted backwards, soaking up the energy.

Lovelace had fought before, Slocum reasoned. Drunk or not, he wasn't going to be easy. He drew in a breath, stalked his prey, followed up with a feint. He started a punch with his right hand, pulled it, then hooked a left under Lovelace's guard, caught him under the left armpit. Lovelace countered with two left jabs, bouncing them off Slocum's left temple.

Slocum shook his head, raised his left shoulder, and quartered in on Lovelace as the men in the saloon crowded around, forming a large circle. They watched with glittering eyes as Slocum drove in a right to Lovelace's midsection, followed with a left cross that crunched into the drunk's jawbone like a mallet striking a hollow gourd.

Lovelace cried out in pain, shook his head, and swung a roundhouse right that grazed Slocum's forehead. Slocum shoved a table aside, came in low, shielding his face with his fists. He hammered two hard lefts into Lovelace's gut, felt the springy muscles of the abdomen give. Lovelace let out a whoosh of air, doubled over. Slocum peppered the outlaw's jaw with two short right jabs.

Wheezing for air, Lovelace staggered backwards, stopped when he hit the wall. Men scrambled out of the way. Slocum stepped in close, two paces, and swayed there, fists cocked to throw. Lovelace glared at Slocum with slitted eyes, muttered something under his breath. When he came off the wall, he was pumping his arms. Slocum let him come on, then sidestepped at the last moment. He drove a hard right into the side of Lovelace's face and the sound was like a maul striking an apple.

Lovelace went down on one knee, a rip along his cheekbone where Slocum's knuckles had cracked the flesh. Blood streamed from the cut. Melanie screamed as Lovelace rose to his feet, swayed to and fro like a wounded bear. He let out a roar of pain and fury and tackled Slocum at the knees. Slocum crashed into a table, went down.

Lovelace swarmed over the big man, flailing him with fists. Slocum felt the man's hot breath on his face as he wriggled to get out from underneath. He kicked hard, and Lovelace's face contorted in a grimace of pain as the tip of Slocum's boot drove into his groin. He let out a screech of pain. Slocum scrambled to his feet, braced himself on the flats of his soles.

When Lovelace got up, Slocum drew back his right

hand and slammed it straight into Lovelace's jaw. Pain shot
through his wrist, up his forearm as he followed through.
Lovelace's eyes rolled in the backs of their sockets and he
threw up his hands as his feet went out from under him.

Lovelace went down and Slocum jumped forward,
stood over him, fists at the ready.

Panting hard, Lovelace shook his head, put out an arm
to steady himself. He struggled to rise.

"You get up again, I'll knock you through the floor,"
said Slocum, his breath coming in hard, short gasps.

"I—I ain't finished yet," said Lovelace. Blood drenched
his face and his eyes tried hard to focus.

"Yes, you are," said Slocum.

"Get up, Jack. You can lick him," said a man from the
edge of the circle.

Jack got up.

Slocum sighed, stepped in close as Lovelace brought up
his guard. Lovelace saw it coming, but there was nothing
he could do about it. He opened his mouth in surprise, but
still Slocum's fist came on. Slocum threw it from behind
his right ear and it was the best right cross he had ever
delivered. His fist cracked off Jack's jaw and the minute he
landed, he knew Lovelace would not be getting up again.

Lovelace went down like a sack of meal. He crumpled
as his knees gave way and collapsed onto the floor in a
heap. Slocum stood over him, his lungs raw-burned as he
sucked wind.

Melanie rushed to her father's side, crouched over him.

She looked up at Slocum.

"You've killed him!" she screamed.

"No, but he'll have some headache when he comes to."

"He was drunk. You had no right to beat him like that."

"He had it coming. Drunk was no excuse. He tried to
tear my head off."

"You're no good," she exclaimed. "You're hateful and mean."

"Yes'm, I am that."

"You didn't have to hit him so hard," she said.

"Yes, I did," said Slocum. "Maybe that's the only way he's going to learn."

"Learn what?"

"That you can't solve big problems with fists. Something's sure eating at your pa. It wasn't me he wanted to beat up in the first place."

"What do you mean?" she asked.

But Slocum didn't answer. He looked at Melanie and saw the understanding in her eyes. If he hadn't stood up when he had, it would have been Melanie lying on the floor, her face battered and bloody.

A silence filled the room, and the circle of men broke up as they went back to their tables.

Slocum reached down, helped Melanie to her feet.

"Anyplace you want to take him?" he asked. "I'll help you if you want."

"I don't want you help," she snapped. But that look of understanding passed between them once again.

Slocum shrugged.

"Maybe you do," he said. "Maybe you will. I'll be around if you need me."

He walked back to his table, dropped a cartwheel on the table, and touched a finger to the brim of his hat as he looked at the bartender.

He could feel her looking at him, feel her stare burning into the back of his neck as he left the saloon, walked out into the night.

5

Slocum almost missed the man in the shadows, but he saw him duck back between the two buildings just before he crossed the street to the hotel. So, that answered that. He was being watched. Skaggs and his bunch wanted to keep an eye on him.

"You there," he called. "I'm going to crawl into my bedroll for the night."

No answer.

Slocum smiled, stepped onto the boardwalk. The street was deserted. He took one last look, went inside, got his key from the desk.

"Good night, Mr. Slocum," said the clerk.

"Good night."

The room was functional. That was about all he could say for it. A bed, a dresser with one short leg, a small table, two chairs. A chamber pot glistened in one corner; there was a pitcher and bowl atop the dresser. He opened

one window a crack, pulled the shade down. The lamplight
flickered, sent a column of oily smoke upwards. The
smoke sprawled across the ceiling, turned invisible against
the black that was already there.

Slocum took off his shirt, felt the spongy pucker of the
old bullet wound high on his chest. It was an unconscious
act, bringing back memories of the shot that collapsed one
lung, drove the air out of it like a squeezed bellows. It
didn't bother him much except on cold nights, but he remembered how close he had come to dying in the spring of
sixty-five, far from his boyhood home in Calhoun County,
Georgia. The wound didn't hurt now, but sometimes it did,
and he took the pain as a sign of his own mortality.

There was an ugly slash mark on his belly, white as
bone, where a breed tried to gut him that time in Socorro.
His back was laced with the marks of the jailer's whip,
broad stripes where the skin had parted under the brutal
force of the lash.

Slocum sat down, stretched his six-foot-one frame out,
and listened to the sounds of the night filtering through the
window. Someone was plucking at the strings of a guitar,
and the notes were distorted, wobbly, but reminded him of
days gone by when he had stopped by wagon trains heading west, listened to homesick talk, and felt a kinship with
people he had never seen before, would never see again.

The sound of voices drifted through the window, and he
heard footsteps crunch on the street below. He looked at
the bed, flexed his back muscles. His shoulder blades were
strong, used to hard ground, but the bed would be welcome
this night. He wondered if was not tempting fate one time
too many by staying in Pipestone. He should be riding on,
maybe up to the Musselshell or the Powder, where he
would sleep with the scent of spruce and balsam in his
nostrils, looking up at the stars and wondering once again

at the mystery of the skies, feeling small and insignificant in the deepness of the heavens.

But there was a mystery here, too, in a town built by outlaws, and something tugged at him to stay, to see what cards came out of the deck. It would not be easy to leave. He would have to shoot his way out and the numbers alone guaranteed that he wouldn't make it. Not yet. Not tonight, nor tomorrow.

Slocum pulled off his boots, tossed them toward the bed. They landed with twin thunks and he stood up, unstrapped his gunbelt, buckled it into a loop, and hung it on the bedpost before he peeled out of his trousers. He turned down the lamp and crawled onto the bed, wearing only his shorts and socks, heard the wooden slats groan with the strain of his weight. He ran fingers through his shock of coal-black hair and closed his eyes. The tiredness drained out of him, and the fog of sleepiness filled his brain, smothered his thoughts.

The tapping broke into the murky dream, and Slocum awakened with a start. It took him a moment to shake off the feeling of disorientation, realize where he was. He looked at the dim outlines of the room, focused on the table, shifted his glance to his gunbelt. He snaked the Colt Navy from the holster, sat up. The tapping grew louder and he realized that someone was at the door.

He padded across the room, listened to the light taps as if to reassure himself that his ears had not deceived him.

"Who's there?" he growled.

"It's me, Melanie Lovelace. Please. Open the door."

"Who's with you?" He had a vision of her father standing behind her, a loaded gun in his hand.

"I'm alone," she whispered through the door.

Slocum slipped the latch, opened the door. He stood

behind it, thumb on the hammer of his Navy Colt. Melanie was alone. Before he could stop her, she rushed quickly into the room. He closed the door, latched it.

Melanie did not look at Slocum right away, but took a wooden sulphur match from her small purse and lit the lamp. When she turned around, she saw Slocum standing there, his naked flesh bronzed by the lampglow.

"Oh, my," she breathed.

"You don't give a man much chance to get decent."

"I—I'm sorry. I didn't think. It's just that I had to talk to you."

"What's on your mind?" he asked.

"You almost make me forget," she said wistfully. Her glance roamed over his body, lingered on his powerful torso, the flat belly, the slim hips. Slocum's mouth twisted in a wry smile.

"You still mad at me, ma'am?"

"No, no, of course not," she said quickly. "At first I was. Because of the drubbing you gave my pa. But, you were right, I guess. He had it coming."

"He beat you a lot?"

"Yes, but he doesn't mean it. He's always sorry afterwards."

"Man who beats a woman always says that. One of these days, he'll go too far."

"What do you mean?" she asked.

"He'll kill you," said Slocum. His eyes narrowed to slits, glittered sea-green in the lampglow. Melanie, taken aback, put a hand to her mouth, gasped in surprise.

"You can't mean that," she said.

"Look, Melanie, I've seen men like Lovelace before. Wife beaters, drunks, kid slappers. They like to pick on people weaker than themselves. Maybe they don't start out hating, but they end up that way. They get to feeling bad about knocking their kids or their wives around and they just get worse. I saw the look in your pa's face. He's gone beyond slapping. If you ever spoke up to him while he was in a rage, he'd kill you. He'd be sorry as hell afterwards, but you'd still be dead."

Melanie slumped down in a chair and sighed deeply. She seemed to sag with an invisible weight on her shoulders. Slocum felt sorry for her.

"You just don't know how hard it's been since Ma died," she said. "I've tried hard to change Pa's ways, but he won't listen to me. He's stubborn and he drinks too much, but he only got that way after Ma died. He blames himself and he keeps trying to drown his troubles in strong drink."

Slocum walked over to the bed, lay down on his back.

"How did your ma die?" he asked softly. He lay in shadow, outside the circle of light thrown by the flickering lamp.

"She was kicked to death by a horse. We had a small ranch up in the Gallatin Valley. The work was hard, too hard, and Ma took too much on herself. One morning she went to feed Pa's stallion and one of the mares came in heat. Poor Ma, she just got in the way of that stallion and Pa, he liked to have gone crazy after that. He shot the horse and took to drinking. He just lost all interest in the ranch after that. He sold off everything and spent all the money, then took up with Emmett Skaggs. When they come to Pipestone, I come along with Pa. I don't like it here, but I'm hopin' I can change my pa's ways."

"You can't," said Slocum gently.

"I could if you'd help me."

"I can't help you."

"You seem to be the only one who understands Pa. I don't know why, but that's the truth of it."

"Then you ought to know one man can't change another, Melanie."

"I—I heard you were a good man. I wanted to make friends with you, but you started asking all those questions and I got scared."

"But now you're not scared anymore," he said.

"A little."

"All right. What do you want me to do?"

"First of all, I want to know if you're going to work for Emmett."

"No."

"But he'll probably ask you to ride with him. And if you don't, he'll kill you."

"Is that the way it is?"

"I—I don't know," she stammered. "I think so. Please, I can't say much right now. But there is someone who can tell you an awful lot."

"Who would that be?" he asked.

"Pete Anders. He's a shopkeeper in town. I think he wants to see you."

"What makes you think that?"

"I've been talking to some people. Not everyone here in town goes along with Emmett, you know."

Slocum wondered if she had talked to Rufus Harding. He wasn't going to press it. Melanie was obviously scared, but she was a woman in trouble. She needed help. And he still wanted to get to the bottom of the mystery of Pipestone. Skaggs apparently ruled with an iron fist and he held a great amount of control over the inhabitants of Pipestone. Slocum wanted to know how and why.

"I'll talk to Anders. You're the second person here who's mentioned his name."

"Be careful," she said, and Slocum realized that she had risen from her chair and was standing by the bed. He opened his eyes, looked up at her. Even in the shadows, he could still see her beauty. She looked like a fine sculpture silhouetted in the lamp's copper glow.

"I will," he said, and felt a tug of desire in his loins.

Melanie began to unbutton the back of her frock. She dropped her handbag on the floor, and slipped out of her dress.

"Pa has kept the men away from me," she said. "Ever since Ma died. I never was alone with a man before."

"Maybe you shouldn't be alone with one now."

"No," she husked. "I—I don't know what it is, but it's as if I've been waiting for you a long time. The moment I saw you, I knew you were different. I don't even want any of the men who work for Emmett. I wouldn't have done anything, even if Pa had let me."

She tugged at her slip and stood there in the puddle of clothes, naked. The light from the lamp seemed to bathe her in its aura, its autumn glow, limning her with the gold of a western sunset, painting her breasts with russet and amber hues, daubing her smooth flesh with delicate tones of auburn.

Slocum wanted her and he knew that she wanted him. The way she stood there, one leg slightly cocked over the other, her hips slightly out of alignment, her breasts jutting proudly from her chest, her hips thrust forward boldly, made his blood stir, made his loins boil with the fresh heat of desire.

"Christ," said Slocum, and his voice was laden with husk and wonder.

"I want you," she said, and came to him, came to him like a woman should come to a man and he took her in his arms and scented the musk of her until it filled his nostrils and made him heady with want and need and all the full-ness of woman-thoughts that had haunted him on the long empty trail coming to this place in the mountains.

He brought her to him, and held her close and she held close to him with her slender arms and he felt her fingers grasp at his back and knead his flesh until he knew that her hunger was the same as the hunger he had in his heart and loins. He rubbed her back, too, and roamed over her backbone and over the arcs of her thighs and wanted more of her, wanted to grasp her closer to him until they were not two people anymore, but just one, coupled, for just a moment and for eternity as well.

"Oh my," she gasped, and her back arched so that he felt the bony ridge of her backbone. She was like delicate china in his hands, like a sleek cat stretching. "You do things to me."

"You do things to me, too," he said, and they kissed as he turned her over on her back.

She lay there submissive until he dipped down to her and then she spread her legs and he slid over her, moving between them until he was poised to enter the swollen lips. He saw the wild flare in her eyes and then he slid his manhood into her and saw the flames dull and her eyes go smokey like two snuffed candles. He sank into her and felt her legs twitch and her muscles contract so that she squeezed him and made the pleasure even greater.

"Oh, yes," she sighed, "yes, Slocum, yes."

He knew what she meant and he pushed inward until he felt the resistance of her maidenhead, felt the twinge that coursed through her body. He backed off and stroked her slow, probing the leathery membrane, pushing harder each time he touched it until he felt it give.

"Does it feel good to you?" she breathed.

"Yes," he said, and pushed again at the virgin's barrier.

"I don't care if it hurts," she said.

"It might hurt some. Like a sting, I've heard tell."

"I've heard it's like being cut with a hot knife."

"Who told you that?"

"My ma."

Slocum laughed, but not at her. "She was trying to scare you," he said.

"Well, she did. Until now." She hunched her hips up hard and quick against him, and the move surprised him. She began to move them, in small circles, grinding away on the shaft of his peg until he felt his loins burn. Fresh blood rushed into the veins of his manhood and it swelled inside her.

He plumbed her depths with renewed force, pushing against the membrane of her girlhood with strong thrusts. She winced with the power of his penetration, but her hips continued to undulate as he skewered her. Theirs was a love dance now, as their bodies melded together, flesh flowing into flesh until they were one person, each perfectly complementing the other.

"Yes, yes," she breathed, and beads of perspiration stood on her forehead, just above her upper lip. Her eyes glittered with the madness of desire. Slocum pushed through the hymen, parting the membrane. She cried out, and her fingernails dug into his back. He plunged past the shorn maidenhead, deep into the virginal tunnel, clear to the mouth of her womb.

"It's over," he said.

"I know," she sighed. "I'm a woman now."

"Yes, Melanie, you are."

He took her with tender savagery until she screamed softly in his ear. Her body bucked with pleasure and she shook with tremors that coursed her flesh like electric lightning. He burrowed through her with a desperate need and her back arched into a graceful bow as the excitement took her, ravished her senses, plundered her willing flesh.

"Oh, oh, oh," she screamed, and her galvanized body thrashed on the bed like a wounded animal.

Slocum could no longer stay his seed. She felt him coming and dug in her fingernails, rammed her hips against his in preparation for the final release.

"Let me have it," she pleaded, and Slocum exploded.

Melanie, jolted with a sudden, unexpected orgasm, cried out in mindless joy. She bucked and quaked with the sizzling energy of climax, and climaxed again in a series of shuddering explosions that rippled through her body like bolts of raw lightning.

"Oh, my, yes," she sobbed and crumpled under him as he collapsed inside her, spent, sated from the final exertion.

"It doesn't get any better than that," he said, rolling from her damp, sweat-sodden body.

"Oh, John, thank you, thank you."

"You needn't thank me," he said.

"It was so beautiful, so wonderful. You make me feel whole. Complete." She stroked his forearm with her hand, brushed the stippled hairs with a gentle touch.

"Ah, yes," Slocum sighed, and lay back like a conquering giant, stretched out his legs.

"I won't ever forget you," she whispered into his ear.

Slocum said nothing, but closed his eyes and ringed her shoulders with his arm, pulled her against him.

"Will you let me sleep with you?" she asked.

"You might not get much sleep."

"I don't care. I don't want to go back to a cold bed. Not now."

"What about your pa?"

"I think you broke much more than my maidenhead," she said softly.

"Yeah, maybe that's so," he mused.

"I want to stay, John."

"Stay, then," he said, and he felt her hand on his limp manhood, felt her fingers touch the sleek flesh.

In a few minutes he wanted her again.

6

Slocum watched Emmett Skaggs and his men ride out of Pipestone. None but Harding and Bonstall had spoken to him, and they with sheepish looks on their faces. When the dust settled, Slocum was once again an outcast, and two men had been left behind to see that he didn't leave town. They each carried loaded shotguns and Slocum knew he wouldn't get five yards if he tried to run away. He shrugged, turned on his heel, followed by the two shadows on either side of the street.

Since he could not go anywhere without being followed, and he couldn't leave town without having to brace two or more hardcases, Slocum figured he'd better make the best of the time on his hands. He didn't want to cause undue attention to his movements, however, so he ambled from building to building, sat for a while on a wooden bench outside the hotel, looked in a window or two, and finally went inside Pete Anders's store. The two shadows stayed outside, but one of them watched through the window and Slocum saw him take his bandana from around his neck and wipe his forehead. Let the bastard sweat, he thought.

The store was nearly empty when Slocum entered. He heard women's voices coming from some back room. A man stood on a small ladder putting airtights on a high shelf back of the counter. Another man pushed a wide broom across the floor, sent motes of dust into the columns of light that beamed through the windows.

"Help you?" asked the man on the ladder without turning around. Slocum's boots rang hollow on the thin hardwood flooring.

"Maybe," said Slocum, "if you're Pete Anders."

"I am. Who's asking?"

"John Slocum." His voice boomed deep and resonant. The man with the broom stopped pushing it and blinked as he looked at the tall green-eyed man from Georgia.

Pete Anders shoved a can of green beans onto the shelf and turned around, looked downward at Slocum. He was a tanned, wiry man with a deep chest, thick, muscled shoulders, hair that was almost white, dark brown eyes, a strong straight nose. He wore an apron, but that did not bely his manliness. He looked as rugged as any man Slocum had ever seen, with corded muscles roping his forearms and a brawny torso atop sturdy legs encased in tight duck trousers.

"You're Slocum, eh?"

"I reckon so."

A slow smile broke on Pete's face, paralleled his square jaw. "Been wonderin' if you'd come around."

"Is there someplace we can talk?" asked Slocum.

"Riley, you go on back and start opening the crates of that new stock that come in," Anders said to the broompusher. Riley, a lean, stringbean young man with unkempt dark hair nodded somberly, pushed his broom over to the wall, and leaned the handle against a shelf. He walked to the back, disappeared through a door. The women's conversation faded away for a moment, then picked up again.

"Come on, Slocum, let's find a spot over by the stove and set a spell."

Anders climbed down from the ladder, led the way down an aisle between stacks of dry goods, blankets, trousers, shirts. He did not have much stock in the store, Slocum noticed, but the goods were all useful, virtually necessary to any civilized community. Beyond the aisles, there was a corner Slocum hadn't noticed, an open place with a pot-bellied stove, half a dozen chairs, a spittoon, a table with a pair of ashtrays fired from native clay.

"Sometimes the boys come in here on cool nights to sit and swap lies," said Anders, waving Slocum to a chair. Anders sat down, dug through a shirt pocket for his pipe, a pouch of tobacco. He filled the bowl, tamped the tobacco down with his thumb, fished a match from another pocket, struck it under the chair seat, and touched it to the tobacco. He drew on the pipe until the tobacco caught. He batted the smoke away, looked at Slocum who sat quietly opposite him, a position that allowed him to watch the front door and the back.

That slow smile broke on Anders's face again.

"You're some used to this, aren't you, Slocum?" he asked.

"What's that?" drawled Slocum.

"Gunplay. Matching wits against the odds. Fighting. Running."

"I never thought of a gun as being used for play," said Slocum.

Anders sucked on his pipe, the corner of his mouth still wrinkled in that half smile of his. A smile, Slocum thought, like the way the smoke curled from his pipe and painted empty space, or the way the wind shaped snow-drifts and left shadows that were not there before. A most interesting man, yet deceptive, like a deep, high mountain lake that was sometimes blue, sometimes green, and had no bottom.

"A play on words, as Shakespeare might have said. Or maybe he did say it that way."

"You're a talker, Anders," said Slocum. "Right enough. But you got anything to say?"

"I got plenty to say, Slocum. I just want to be damned sure I say it to the right man. This town's got a lot of secrets. No, it was damned sure built on secrets. And I've seen men change like the weather, every twenty minutes, even men you thought you could trust."

"That's real good general information. Hell, I could have told you that five minutes after I walked into town."

"Look, Slocum, I'm probably wrong in even talking to you, but sometimes I play my hunches. I could get killed for saying too much and I don't know you from Bunyan's blue ox."

"You could get killed for not saying anything, too," observed Slocum. "Evenutally, Skaggs is going to start counting real close friends, and my bet is you won't be among 'em."

Anders's eyes narrowed as he regarded Slocum more shrewdly than before.

"You ain't mealy-mouthed, are you now?"

"I step careful, but I don't flap my jaw at the wrong times."

"I'm wondering why you came back after you got your goods back from those Injuns."

"I'm wondering the same thing, Anders. And what

about you? What keeps you in Pipestone? Money? The fresh air?"

"You know something, Slocum? You ought to practice up your sarcasm. It ain't near good enough to rub any hide off my back."

"I'll try," said Slocum. "Meantime, I heard you were your own man and wouldn't mind telling me more about Pipestone and Skaggs."

"Ah. Well, Pipestone, it's a hidey-hole town, an outlaws' roost, a town perched on the edge of Hell. I didn't exactly pick it out as a place to live, you know. Me, I can think of dozens of other places I'd rather be right now."

Anders had the peculiar habit of tugging on his right earlobe and then tweaking the tip of his nose as if he had once dipped snuff. He practiced this odd mannerism at every pause in the conversation.

"How'd you end up here?" asked Slocum.

"You ever been to the Gulches?"

"Been through 'em. Alder and Grasshopper."

"I mined 'em both, not so far back, but I came to this country around the time that Red River half-breed Benetsee found gold in Deer Lodge Valley. Came out before the Stuarts, even. Warn't many people here, then, a few old trappers who hadn't give up, some traders what had wed squaws. We all lived like Injuns then. Well, it was a pretty good way to live. I was a young buck, full of piss and vinegar. There was times when I wished I had me some bread and coffee, some sugar, but I could speak some Injun, whipsaw lumber, blacksmith, butcher beef and buffalo.

"I built me a cabin for my family. There was my wife, Julie, and my daughter, Sally, my sister, Alice. Julie, she died, and Alice married a man named Cummings. He died, too, but Alice, she helped raise Sally and they both work here in the store, bless 'em.

"I raised some cattle and grew some grain, trapped. We lived. Then, we heard about the War when we was up on the American Fork, but warn't nothin' we could do about it. You was in the War?"

"I was."

"South, I reckon." Anders pulled his right earlobe, then grasped the tip of his nose between his thumb and index finger, sniffed air into his nostrils. He didn't seem to be aware of the mannerism.

"Yes," said Slocum.

"Don't matter no more. It's over and done with, I reckon. We had us some times. Back in sixty-two, we started off the new year with a real wing-ding over at John Grant's place. He had him a grand ball. Most of the ladies were Injun or had Injun blood. They was dressed in calico bright as new gold, scarlet leggins, beaded moccasins, all wrapped in plaid blankets and festooned with silver ornaments. The party lasted three days because a blizzard come up and there warn't no place else to go. Them two fiddlers made the boards buck, I tell you. We had a breakfast feast on New Year's Day and then all went to bed in our clothes, a-lyin' on buffalo robes in Johnny Grant's house. We ate dinner at two that afternoon and then danced some more until nine when we had some more supper. That blizzard never let up until January third. We ate another big breakfast and rode home in the cold, the snow fourteen feet deep if it was an inch. Oh, we had us some times."

"So, you tried for the gold," said Slocum.

"I did, and then I got a little smart. I turned to shop-keeping and did some grubstaking. When the gold played out, Skaggs come along and made me an offer. I didn't know much about him, then, but like a fool, I finally helped him build Pipestone."

"Did you know then that Skaggs was an outlaw?"

"I reckon I wanted to think he was just another horse-trader."

"But, you knew," persisted Slocum.

"Not right off. Time I found out, it was too damned late." Once again, Anders pulled on his earlobe, sniffed as he pinched his nose-tip. He did this so quickly, a less observant person than Slocum might not have noticed it.

Before Slocum could question Anders further, a pretty girl came out of the back, followed by a woman who was slightly older.

"Pa, what are you doing?" asked the girl, a look of seriousness on her face.

"Just jawin'," said Anders sheepishly.

"I could hear you," she said. "You'd best keep still."

"Now, hold on, Sally. This here's Mr. John Slocum, and he's not one of Skaggs's bunch."

Sally, a slender, dark-haired woman with nut-brown eyes, slender, waspish waist, and trim ankles, looked at Slocum, open-mouthed. The woman behind her, taller, of graceful bearing, had the same straight nose as Anders, the same dark brown eyes. Her light sandy hair was swept back away from her face. She looked fresh-scrubbed, intelligent, headstrong.

"This here's my daughter, Sally, and my sis, Alice Cummings."

"Pete," said Alice, "you'd best look over the inventory we've prepared." She spoke crisply and tried her best to ignore Slocum's presence.

"Don't mollycoddle me, Alice. This here's a friend."

"I'm sure," said Alice. "Please excuse us, Mr. Slocum," she said. "My brother has work to do."

Anders stood up, his face flushed.

"Now, hold on, Alice. You don't understand—"

Alice walked up to her brother, then, and Slocum was struck with her regal glide, the smooth way she walked. She looked her brother square in the eyes and spoke in an audible whisper.

"Pete, this isn't funny. You know nothing about this man. He could be one of Emmett's spies."

There it was, thought Slocum. Out in the open. Even the good people of Pipestone looked on him with suspicion. He felt very uncomfortable just then, but this was something Anders had to work out with his sister and daughter. He thought he detected fear in Sally's wide-eyed stare and not a little in Alice's urgent whispers to her brother.

"I'll be getting along," said Slocum. "Sorry I bothered you, Anders."

"Wait, you ain't botherin' me. Look, I got a lot more to say, but I got to talk to my women. Can you come by the house tonight, after we're closed up?"

"What about my shadows out there?"

"Maybe you can dodge 'em," said Anders.

"I don't want to get you into trouble," said Slocum. Alice Cummings looked at him impatiently. Sally frowned. Slocum rose from his chair, but he didn't make a move to leave. Alice begin to tap one foot on the floor. The sound irritated Slocum. It was soft, but insistent, like a water drip on a flat rock.

"No—no, I don't think Emmett would say anything. He's got a reason for lettin' you stay in town. Maybe he'll make you an offer pretty quick."

"Maybe," said Slocum, his heart hammering in his chest. "Any chance of that?"

"I don't know. He'll look you over a long time, the way

he does with the men he picks, but if you don't make him suspicious, he may give you a try."

"And what should I do about that if he does?" asked Slocum.

"Well, I can't say," said Anders, doing the tweak and tug with his fingers, "but once you get in with Skaggs, it's damned hard to get out."

"Pa," pleaded Sally.

"Pete, we *really* do need you in the back," said his sister, giving Slocum another sharp look. Slocum touched a finger to the brim of his hat, smiled.

"See you ladies tonight," he said softly.

Alice drew herself up indignantly and Sally's mouth opened wide in surprise.

"How dare . . ." began Alice Cummings.

"Shut up," said Pete Anders, grinning wide. "You come for supper, John Slocum. The gals will set you a plate. About seven, I reckon. Buy you a drink."

"I'll be there," said Slocum, matching Anders's grin. He tipped his hat to the ladies and stalked across the room, walked out the door. He heard the babble of female voices rise up behind him as he closed the door.

Slocum looked at the man waiting outside, slouched against the side of the building.

"Come on, son," he said, "let's go find someplace to sit where it's cool."

"Slocum, you ain't half as smart as you think you are," said the man.

"Well, I reckon that's smart enough, then," said Slocum.

The erstwhile guard didn't laugh. Slocum walked across the street, headed for the saloon. The other man came out of the shadows on the other side of the street, squinted into the sun, blinked.

Now, thought Slocum, was as good a time as any to give these two jaspers the slip. He was tired of their unwanted company.

Jethro Dekins drank his warm beer, wished for something stronger. But, he had a job to do, orders from Emmett. Slocum was to be watched, kept track of, not allowed to leave Pipestone. His partner for the chore, Nate Wales, shared the pail of bitter brew, smoked endless quirlies that he kept rolling and lighting as if that would quell his nervousness.

Dekins was the man who had stood outside the door of Pete's general store while Slocum had been inside. He was still rankling over the words the stranger had spoke to him. Deke didn't like the name of Jethro and no one who knew him well called him that.

"Nate, I hope that pilgrim turns in early, so he don't have to turn in dead."

"Deke, you worry too goddamned much. Slocum's just a-tryin' to get your goat, is all. He ain't nobody much to fret over. Look at him, a-standin' at the bar, swillin' down hard likker. He'll fold like a army tent in a windstorm 'fore the sun falls down."

"The man's a curly wolf, Nate. He don't go the grain. Hell, you're nervous as a long-tail in a room full of rockin' chairs yourself."

"Yeah, maybe, but I got five beans in the wheel what will stop him dead he makes a move to light a shuck."

Dekins put the glass to his lips, drank half of the stinging brew. He wiped a thin line of foam from his lips. He was a beetle-browed, square-jawed man with little sense of humor. He had small, deepset eyes that held a permanent squint behind high cheekbones. Some said he had Cherokee blood in his veins, but anyone who mentioned it was liable to get a fist in his face, or a pistol barrel laid across the side of his head.

Nate was slender, tow-haired as a kid, and looked at the world with pale blue eyes that were almost gray. His eyes, in fact, appeared lifeless, devoid of emotion. He wore a washed-out moustache under his flat nose. Men who looked at him close stepped aside when he walked near. He had that look of the killer, and he wore his sixgun low on his belt. Few knew that he carried another behind his back, tucked there within easy reach. The man seemed dull and uninterested in his surroundings, but a careful look revealed that he missed very little. He was shy and talked little, but he had a hunger look on his face and he licked his lips all the time as if he wanted to taste blood.

Slocum seemed not to notice the two men sitting at the table, watching him, but he observed them at intervals, out of the corners of his green eyes. He knew what kind of men they were, and he knew that they would try to kill him if he made a wrong move. But, knowing them, he knew their weaknesses, as well.

"Buy the boys a drink," he told the barkeep. "A pail of beer, cool as you got."

"Beer's hotter'n a two-dollar pistol on the fourth of July," cracked the bartender. "I put a wet cloth over the clay jug, but my beer still bites back."

"Good enough," said Slocum softly, and plunked coin down on the bar.

The bartender took the pail of beer over to the table of the two hardcases. Slocum turned to them and smiled, touched his hand to the brim of his hat in mock salute.

Nate and Deke stiffened as the barkeep bowed to tell them that Slocum had bought them the bucket of beer. Wary, they floated hands down close to their pistols, looked at Slocum closely.

Slocum grinned and turned back to the bar, seemingly unconcerned.

Out of the corner of his eye, he saw the two hardcases relax. They began to drink the beer he had sent over to them. Slocum moved down the bar, toward the back of the saloon, a few inches at a time. When the other two looked away from him, he took several quick strides, opened the back door and disappeared outside, leaving the door wide open.

He climbed the stairs of the building next door, crawled by a window, and gained the roof of the false front. He hunkered down there, waited.

The two men dashed outside the saloon, their pistols drawn. They looked up and down the alleyway.

"Nate, you go that way," said Deke. "I'll go the other."

"Just so's we find him," said Nate.

"The bastard can't be far. Meet you at the stables."

The two men dashed off in opposite directions. Slocum waited until he no longer heard them, then crawled back to the top of the stairs. He walked down, across the alley, and kept going until he reached a stand of firs back of the town. He concealed his tracks, crawled under a big blue spruce, and took off his hat. He lay down and closed his eyes. The trees muffled all sounds from the town of Pipestone. As he drifted off to sleep, it seemed that he was all alone, free again, taking a rest from the trail.

7

It was still light out when Slocum awoke from his nap. He heard men calling, heard hoofbeats of horses riding up and down Pipestone's lone main street. He heard the banging of doors, the angry shouts, the curses.

So, he thought, the two hardcases were still looking for him. He crawled from under the spruce tree, brushed himself off. He held three fingers up to the horizon, just below the sun. Half an hour until dark, another half hour and he could find his way to Pete Anders's place and supper. He smiled. He could have been a long way from Pipestone by now, if he'd been on horseback. As it was, he was still a prisoner, but the terms were getting a little better.

Slocum had a picture of the town in his mind, now, and he fixed the place that Anders called home, went to it by dead reckoning. It was turning dark when he found the place, a log cabin with a sod roof that smelled like heaven. The smell of beef cooking wafted on the evening air and

67

Slocum's stomach churned with a sudden hunger pang. The windows were unshuttered and copper light spilled from the openings, splashed on the ground outside. Bats darted through the shadowy air on the fringes of the light, slicing through the insects that bounced up and down like moonbeams on water. From inside the house, Slocum heard the mournful whine of a harmonica, the creak of a rocking chair.

The tall man took a turn around the house, staying to the deepening shadows, stopping every so often to listen, his green eyes piercing the darkness, searching for any sign of movement, anything out of place. It was quiet, except for the keen of the harmonica, and Slocum stepped up to the back porch, pushed on the door. It was unlatched and swung open. He stepped inside, walked down the short hall toward the lantern light, the heavy scent of food on the cookstove.

Alice Cummings saw him as he strode into the kitchen, his large frame blocking the doorway for a moment. She let out a little cry and clutched her neck. Sally Anders cried "Oh," and jumped back from the stove, a large, wooden-handled spoon in her hand.

"Sorry, ladies," said Slocum, "I didn't want to attract attention by banging on your back door."

"Well, you gave us a start, Mr. Slocum," said Alice, a stern look of annoyance on her face. Steam had relaxed a few strands of hair that dangled becomingly down both sides of her face. The light caught the glint in her eyes. She wore a pretty frock with a square-cut yoke that revealed the barest tops of her breasts pushing against the fabric.

"My apologies for getting your blood up."

"Why, yes. Go on, then, now that you're here. My brother is expecting you."

"Smells mighty nice," he said, touching a finger to the

brim of his hat. He looked at Sally, who stood frozen by
the stove, the spoon held aloft in her white-knuckled hand.
She, too, was dressed right smart, in a gingham dress that
clung to her like a glove. Her face began to take on the
color it had lost when he made his unexpected entrance.

The harmonica stopped playing and Slocum headed
down the hall, past closed bedroom doors. He entered the
front room, saw Pete Anders sitting in the rocking chair, a
silver harmonica in his hand. It gleamed in the glow of
lamplight, bounced light like a signal mirror.

"Thought I heard voices," said Pete. "Set yourself in a
chair, Slocum."

Slocum took off his hat, sat on a sturdy hard-backed
chair. The smell of pipesmoke almost overpowered the
aroma of food and he saw the pipe resting in a clay *ceni-
cero* like ones he had seen in Santa Fe. The room was
sparsely furnished, but showed the touches of a woman's
hand, flowers in water glasses made to serve as vases,
framed samplers on the log walls, doilies on the divan, the
glistening surface of polished wood everywhere he looked.
A pair of dulcimers hung on the wall, gracefully curved,
the thin walnut polished to a high sheen.

Anders set down the harmonica, picked up his pipe. He
drew on it, and blue smoke coiled from the bowl. It was
good tobacco, cured and scented with apples. He saw,
then, the small glass on the table next to Anders's chair,
filled with an amber liquid. There was an empty glass next
to it, and a bottle underneath the table. Anders leaned over,
picked up the bottle, held it over the thick-bottomed glass.

"Pour you a drink, Slocum?"

"I'll have a taste."

The whiskey sloshed in the glass. Slocum leaned over
as Anders handed him the drink.

"You got Nate and Deke in a dither," said Anders, the

trace of a smile on his face. "They been turnin' this town upside down a-huntin' you."

Anders fiddled with his earlobe, pinched the tip of his nose. Slocum was almost getting used to the habit.

"Hard to find something that's not there," said Slocum.

Anders laughed, slapped his knees. Slocum got the idea that Anders hadn't laughed in a long while. There was something self-conscious about it, almost reserved, as if he was afraid to let his feelings be known. Pete looked around the room, broke off his laugh abruptly.

"You been hiding in the woods, I reckon."

"I have," said Slocum. "Not hiding. I snoozed."

"Them boys come boilin' out of that saloon like hornets from a holler tree when you slipped away from 'em. They raised a hoot 'n' a holler sech as Pipestone ain't never heard. Gave me a tickle to see them chasin' their tails all afternoon."

"They say anything to you?" asked Slocum.

"Ast if I'd seed you. I told 'em no."

"Seems pretty quiet now, in town."

"That's because Harding and Bonstall rode in a while ago. Skaggs and the rest of the bunch will be here by morning. I gather they was some trouble on this trip."

"Oh?"

"Neither Bonstall nor Harding will say anything, but they put away their horses wet. They was lathered pretty well. We'll probably hear all about it by tomorry."

Slocum wondered what might have happened. The only reason he could figure that Harding and Bonstall came in early was because Skaggs was either fighting or trying to throw a posse off his trail. Either way, it meant that Pipestone was likely not as secure as it once was. You couldn't keep a secret like this forever.

Sally came into the front room, stood in the doorway.

"Pa, when do you want us to put supper on?"

"Give us a quarter hour or so, Sally," said her father.

"Perfect," she said, "Alice is making biscuits."

Slocum's stomach wrenched at the thought. Fresh biscuits. The hunger gnawed at him now. He finished off his drink. Sally looked at him, softened.

"Sounds good to hear Pa laugh again," she said, before turning on her heel and leaving the room.

"Yair, I reckon," growled Anders. "Slocum, have another drink and pull up your chair. I got some things in my craw I want to get out and now's as good a time as any."

Anders poured drinks for both of them. Slocum scooted his chair closer to his. He took the drink. The whiskey, though, made him even hungrier. He heard the subdued voices of the ladies coming from the kitchen, and the night sounds from outside as Anders swallowed a healthy slug of whiskey, cleared his throat.

"Them are good women, Slocum. They look after things when I have to go off to Butte and buy supplies. Don't nobody bother them much. I know they live in fear of Skaggs and his bunch ever' damn day of their lives, but they don't complain."

"I don't see why you would keep them here, Anders. It's not a fit place for women. This is a damned robber's roost, for Christ's sake."

"I know, I know," said Pete. "Hell, I don't want 'em here, but they come along and now Skaggs won't let 'em go. We're just as much prisoners here as you are."

"Damned shame," said Slocum.

"Listen, I don't want the women to hear these things and there's a lot I can't tell you, but I got to tell somebody before I choke on it. You seem to be a hard man, but a decent one, and I have a hunch you want to bring Skaggs down if you can. Am I right?"

"Maybe," said Slocum. "I can't do much by myself."

"No, I don't know a man here who would back you, 'lessen you made a pretty big play and got the upper hand right quick. But, they's good men here, too. We had some hopes someone like you would come along and tear Emmett Skaggs a new asshole. But, I don't know. You hear what I got to say, you might just want to get the hell out and save your own hide."

"I'll listen," said Slocum.

"Just before Skaggs packed up and left the Gallatin Valley, some folks were murdered. A whole family. It was known that they had a heap of gold, and Emmett, he heard about it. Him and Bonstall rounded up a bunch of men and they rode out there. Christ, Slocum, they killed old man Crowell, his son Luke and Luke's wife, Mattie, and their three chillun. Folks blamed the damned vigilantes, but it was Skaggs."

"How do you know this?"

"Heard 'em talkin', just before, and right after. I think that's one reason Emmett made me help him build Pipestone, come out here."

"What else?" asked Slocum.

"A deputy marshal come after Skaggs about two months ago. I think he had tracked 'em after they raided a wagon train coming into the territory. This one, he come right into the town, thinkin' it's just like any other town. Rode right up the main street, hitched his horse to the rail in front of the saloon. They was all a-waitin' for him. Emmett, Harding, Jethro Dekins, Nate Wales and Nate Bonstall, a bunch of others. They let this marshal get almost to the door of the saloon and they opened up on him with pistols, Greeners, anything that would shoot. They shot that pore son of a bitch to pieces right in front of ever'body. Christ, it was gory. They dragged his body up and down the street, then took him to the Jefferson and dumped him in the river."

"And no one came after that?"

"Nary a soul," said Anders. Beads of sweat stood out on his forehead. He drank his liquor, did the business with his ear and nose, went on.

"They been rustling cattle and killing, more since they come here," Pete continued. "They been braggin' about it. Ever' time they come back from a raid, the stories get taller. Trouble is, I believe 'em. That bunch has got blood on its hands, and Emmett, he seems to thrive on it. The killin'. And, I'm not talkin' just about growed men, Slocum. He's kilt women and chillun. No witnesses. God, I just get all sick inside when I think of it. Damn, damn, damn."

It was apparent to Slocum that Pete Anders was a much troubled man. He was clearly in anguish, tormented by the deeds he recounted now, afraid some, too, and probably wondering how he could wipe out the nightmare and not lose his life in the process. It was a hell of a horn to have digging into your back, Slocum thought. And he was slowly beginning to piece together the story of Pipestone and the evil men who had built it. Emmett Skaggs was a man who had killed once and gotten away with it. After that, life hadn't meant much to him. Human life, the lives of others.

Slocum had run across such men before. They began to get a feeling of power and once they had that, they were like mad dogs. They killed until someone shot them down, stopped them in their tracks. Skaggs was such a man, and the town had made him bolder. It was a haven, a refuge, a place where he felt safe. More than that, it was a place he ruled as king and emperor. Nobody questioned him. Such power was akin to madness. It drove a man like Skaggs to commit even more atrocities, sure of his impunity from the laws of men.

Slocum wondered if he should try to catch up his horse and ride to Butte, drum up a posse. He couldn't do it alone. Nate Bonstall and Rufus Harding couldn't be counted on for help. At least not yet. They were Skaggs men until someone stronger, harder, came along and put out Emmett's lamp. Well, that was a possibility, too. Maybe.

"Anders," said Slocum, "you gave me a lot to chew on, and I don't have any answers for you right now. Maybe Skaggs is in trouble over this latest raid, maybe not. We'll just have to wait and see."

"I been doin' that a long time," Anders said sadly.

It had been a spell since Slocum had taken supper with two women as pretty as Sally and Alice. He and Pete sat with them at the round table in the kitchen, let the women treat them like lords. Alice sat on Slocum's left, Sally on his right. Sally heaped his plate high with roast beef, mashed potatoes. Alice passed the biscuits, kept warm in a wicker basket with a checkered cloth surrounding them to keep the heat in. There was honey and hot coffee, plenty of sopping gravy, and potatoes from the Gallatin Valley.

"Pretty fair spread for an outlaw town," said Slocum, and he felt Alice's hand on his knee under the table. When he looked at her, he found no expression on her face.

"It pleases us that you find our food to your liking," she said, and her words dripped with meaning. He missed the sharp look that passed between Alice and Sally, but when he turned back to his plate, he felt a hand on his other knee, and the toe of Sally's shoe pushing his trouser leg up over the top of his boot.

Pete Anders ate like a hardrock miner at a Fourth of July

picnic and did not notice the way the two women kept glancing at Slocum. Sally refilled the biscuit basket, and she leaned over Slocum as she set it on the table, brushed his shoulder with her bare arm.

Slocum felt the telltale tug at his loins, the growth that was sudden and unexpected.

"Did Pa tell you all about Pipestone?" asked Sally.

"Some."

"Are you going to help us get out?"

The way she blurted it out, Slocum knew that the women must have been talking about him while they prepared supper. The two women looked at each other, and at Anders, but Pete kept his head down, looked only into his plate.

"That's a hard question," said Slocum. "And not an easy answer for a man in my position."

"And just what is your position, Mr. Slocum?" asked Alice, fixing him with an accusing, wide-eyed stare that was as blunt as the flat of an anvil.

"For the time being," he said, "I'm just as helpless as you all are. I don't know the territory. I don't know anything about Skaggs or his men. They're not breaking the law here."

"Proof? Are you looking for proof?" persisted Alice.

"Not necessarily. I'm not a lawman. There's just more I have to know before I make any plans."

"I see," said Alice, sarcastically. "You're a coward."

Slocum said nothing, but Anders looked up at Slocum. "Don't let my sister get to you," said Pete. "She means well."

"I just don't think John Slocum is man enough to pee standing up," said Alice, rising from the table. She flounced out of the kitchen. A moment later, they all heard the front door slam.

"I'm sorry," said Pete. "Alice has been through a lot. She's pretty danged flustered."

"I reckon," said Slocum. He got up from the table. "Maybe I ought to have a private talk with her."

"Might do some good. You watch her, though. She's got a temper like a wildcat and a short fuse."

Sally opened her mouth to say something, but closed it again wordlessly. Slocum stalked from the kitchen. A moment later, he found Alice standing in the darkness of the front porch, staring out at the starry night. The lamplight from the town cast an orange glow in the sky.

"Leave me be," she said, as he came up to her.

"Be glad to, if you'll hear me out," he said. "I think you've got a wrong brand on me."

"Have I?" she taunted. In the subdued light, she was even more beautiful than before. The shadows softened the lines in her face, the faint glow of light from the window tanned her features with a light touch of gold.

"I'm no hothead that comes in shooting without knowing what the stakes are," he said. "I know you and your family got troubles. Other folks here, too, don't like Skaggs, what he does. Maybe I drifted here for a reason, but I don't know yet."

"You're right, Mr. Slocum, we've got troubles. I heard how you stood up to Melanie's pa, and I heard talk about how you got your horse back. I thought, well, maybe there's a good honest man come here to be our champion, to right what's wrong. I guess I was mistaken."

"That could be," said Slocum. "You shouldn't get your hopes up too high. I'm just one man and there's a bunch to go against if it comes to that."

"As I said, you're a coward."

Slocum's eyes grew flinty in the light, but he swallowed his pride, drew a deep breath. Alice was an exasperating woman. He saw her point of view, but it was narrow and restricted. She didn't see things from his perspective at all. The worst thing he could do now would be to challenge Skaggs in his own lair. The fight would be over before it had begun.

"Alice, you've got to trust me."

"Do I? I've trusted men before. Look where it got me."

"Your brother?"

"Yes," she hissed.

"It's not his fault. He got in over his head. There's not much law out this way and a man's views get warped, like he looks at things through wavy glass. Pete has a conscience, at least, and it's working at him. A man like Skaggs takes advantage of the weak ones. He knows how to work the herd, turn the runners back in."

"Pete's not weak," she protested.

"Against Skaggs, he is."

She turned toward him, then. He smelled the musk of her, the vague wisp of perfume on her body, in her hair.

"Yes," she sighed, "I guess we all are a little weak compared to Emmett Skaggs."

Slocum felt the magnetism of the woman. He felt drawn to her, yet he did not have to move. She came to him, then, just glided close to him and offered the temptation of her lips. He kissed her lightly and the electricity jumped between them. She pressed her loins into his and he took her into his arms, kissed her hard on the lips. She gasped for breath, and put her arms around his neck.

"Oh, John," she sighed, and he tasted the hunger in her mouth as she locked her lips on his and drenched his tongue with her own hot saliva.

Slocum felt the porch rail dig into the small of his back. Alice seemed to want him to take her right there. Her hot breath scorched his face, her loins melded to his, stirred the heat in his groin, stirred desire from deep within him.

The harmonica began to play, and then the dulcimer took up the melody. The music drifted through the window, out onto the porch. Alice broke her hold on Slocum, smoothed her ruffled hair with fluttering hands.

"My," she gasped, "I guess I lost my senses there for a moment."

"No harm done," said Slocum lightly.

"No? Maybe not, but you're going to spend the night, John Slocum."

"Uh, I wasn't invited by your brother."

"Not yet," she said. "But he will. Come, we'd best go inside or they'll be suspicious."

Slocum followed Alice inside the house. Pete sat in his chair, Sally on the divan, the dulcimer across her lap. Alice ambled across the room, took her own instrument down from the wall. She sat beside her niece, picked up the melody, using her index finger as a noter, plucking the strings with her right hand fingers.

Bom, bitty, bitty, bitty, went the beat, while Pete soared with the melody. Alice and Sally took the accompaniment and made the walls of the cabin reverberate with sound.

Slocum began to tap his foot.

A moment later, Sally began to sing one of the songs Slocum remembered, a Kentucky song of heartbreak and infidelity, of wildwood flowers and summer nights. It made him homesick for Georgia, homesick for a place that was no longer his home.

8

Emmett Skaggs was boiling mad. He had lost one man on the raid, two others were wounded. There was blood on his sleeve where he had held Larry Doolin as he lay dying in a stand of timber just on the other side of the Jefferson not four hours ago. Phil Neary and Jack Candless were both shot up. Jack would probably die if the gangrene started on his leg.

Nate Wales hated like hell to tell Emmett that he and Deke had let Slocum get away from them. He licked dry lips and shifted the weight on his feet for the tenth time as he stood in Emmett's kitchen, watching the outlaw leader pull the cork out of a bottle of rye whiskey.

"Well, Nate, what you got to say?" asked Skaggs.

"That Injun killer, he give me and Deke the slip, Emmett."

"Rode out of town, did he?" asked Emmett, his eyes red-rimmed from sand and grit, long hours without sleep.

There was more than an edge of sarcasm to his tone. There was a dangerous venomous lash to his tongue. "Just up and rode out to blabber about what we got here?"

"Well, no, I don't reckon he rode out, and he likely didn't go far, Emmett."

"What in hell do you mean, Wales? Quit your damned sniveling and spit out what you got in your craw."

"I figger he'll sneak back in to town tonight and try to catch him a horse at the stables or somewhere."

"Oh, you do, do you?" Emmett drank the rye from the bottle. The whiskey made a gurgling sound as it fought the air pocket in the neck. Skaggs drank a good half inch of rye before he took the bottle away from his lips, not counting what was in the bottleneck. "And, what in hell have you done to stop him from doing that?"

"Well, now, Deke, he's over to the stables, I got Nate Bonstall watchin' one end of town, Harding the other. I aim to stay handy, my eyes peeled."

"Sit down, Wales," said Skaggs.

Wales sat down. In the next room, Phil Neary lay on a cot, passed out from loss of blood. His shirt was ripped. Part of it was wrapped around his midsection. It was soaked with blood that had partially dried. His face looked waxen in the lamplight.

Skaggs called this place his "war room," and it was sparsely furnished, with a big table, several chairs, a box-like cabinet for liquor and papers. There were several sleeping rooms in Skaggs's house, a large room where he could sit in comfortable chairs and look down at the row of false fronts that bordered one side of Pipestone's main street. It gave him satisfaction to know that he had built a town that he alone ruled, safe from pursuing lawmen or posses, well off the main trails, hidden from casual view. It disturbed him now that one man threatened that security.

"Why do you think Slocum ran out on you?" Skaggs asked evenly. He fixed Wales with a skewering look.

"Hell, I don't know, Emmett. He didn't look like he was a-goin' to go anywheres. He bought us a beer at the saloon and then he lit a shuck."

"Man does something like that, means he don't like our hospitality or else he's got somethin' up his sleeve," said Skaggs, ruminating as he moved his whiskey glass around on the war room table. "Man's plumb devious, you ask me. I been studyin' on him whilst we was out raidin'. Where in hell'd he come from? What's he want. Man comes walkin' in here out of nowhere and Nate Bonstall thinks he's some punkins. All right. Slocum acted pretty smart with them Injuns and that bothers me some, too. Yep, I got to see more of the stuff this Slocum's made of. I want to see what he's got in his innards and what color stripe he's got down his backbone."

Skaggs stared past Wales, into an empty space that might have been the wall, might have been a featureless point on the side of the mountain that rose in the distance, beyond the town. He was looking at nothing outside of him, but he was looking at something in his head, something dark and shadowy in his mind.

"He might be on the owlhoot," ventured Wales. His nervousness showed in the way he kept looking at Emmett's whiskey glass, then up at the grime ring on Emmett's neck, like an obscene totem, never looking him square in the eye, never wanting to get stuck by that hard gaze of Skaggs's.

"He might be runnin'," said Emmett, still in that dreamy, tired voice of his that was like a horse walking on loose gravel, like footsteps crunching on the night earth, all in shadow and secret. "Might be he's found him a home, but don't like bein' hobbled. Hard to tell with a man like that. I talked a lot to Bonstall and Harding this trip, Wales, and I can tell you they're mighty impressed, mighty impressed with Slocum. Yeah, and I got a feelin', too, that the man's been runnin' a long time. Like you know that feller was we had with us once't, what the hell was his name, Sullivan? Sutter?"

"The feller from Tennessee? Sutphen?"

"Yeah, Sutphen. Darrel Sutphen. He comes to us like a whupped pup. Always talkin' about Missionary Ridge and that Cap'n Billy Gunnison and them Tennessee Volunteers. Sorry son of a bitch, Sutphen was. Never trusted no one and always looked over his damned shoulder like someone was a-follerin' him from Hell. The bastard made me nervous, I can tell you. Yeah, Slocum, he's a damned reb, too, and hard tellin' what he lost in the War. Maybe his guts, maybe his balls, maybe his folks, his woman. War does some things to men. Me, I never paid it no mind. I got somethin' out of it, fact is. Foragin', that's what I call it. Hell, folks call it robbin' and stealin' now, but it's just foragin'. Foragin' off the land, eh, Nathan?"

Nate Wales laughed edgily.

"Yair, Emmett, that's how I figger it."

"This Slocum now, he's plenty smart. But I don't trust him. I don't trust no man till I see what brand he wears on his ass. Slocum may be a drifter, a saddle tramp, an owl-hooter. Or he may be some kind of law."

"Naw," said Wales, "I don't think so. I think he just got tired of being follered around and he run off so's he could have a good laugh at us."

Emmett thought about that for a few moments.

He lit a cigar, blew a spool of blue smoke toward the lamp. A shadow passed across his face, lingered around his eyes. The man was tired, Wales could see that. In the next room, Jack Candless groaned loud and long. Emmett

scowled and drew deep on his cigar. He held the smoke in
his lungs and let it out without coughing.

"Somebody give Jack some whiskey," said Skaggs.
"Damn, I hate to hear a man cry like that."

"He's just hurtin'," said Wales, and was sorry he said it.
He still couldn't see Emmett's eyes. He didn't want to, but
they were behind a thin veil of smoke and that made
Skaggs seem even more ominous than he was. "I'll give
him some whiskey directly."

"You better think real hard about this Slocum feller,"
said Skaggs. "He's armed, you know. He could have
jumped you and Deke if he'd had a mind to."

"We thought about that after he run off."

"Yeah, well, you keep thinkin' about it and keep a
finger on the trigger."

"I will," said Wales bitterly.

"He comes back, I want to see him, hear?"

"What you got in mind, Emmett?"

Emmett smiled, but there was no warmth in it. It was a
smile twisted with cruelty and vicious purpose. It made
Wales's insides squeeze up and turn over.

"I'm thinkin' he might want to ride with us next time we
go out foragin'."

"Yeah," said Wales and he walked to the liquor cabinet
and took a bottle off the shelf. Jack Candless was screaming now, and sobbing like a woman having a kid.

Pete Anders drank more whiskey after supper. He drank
while the women played the old songs and sang in their
sweet, high-pitched voices over the ring of the dulcimers.
Slocum did not drink with him, but watched the two
women and thought of old times back in Georgia, before
the War, when the folks got together and played games,
danced, and sang songs. It made him sad to think about

those times, but he was glad he could remember them, could remember when his folks and his brother were still alive, and happy.

"Maybe you just better get out of Pipestone and save your skin," Anders said abruptly, when the girls had finished playing "Barbry Allen."

"Huh?" asked Slocum, jerked suddenly from his reverie.

"It's too late for us, but maybe not for you. I know, you think I'm drunk, but I'm not. My mind is clear. I been thinkin' 'bout this predicament a long time, Slocum. Me 'n' the gals know we can't get out of Pipestone. Even if I snuck 'em out in the wagon and drove a hunnert miles, Skaggs would find us."

"How do you know?" Slocum asked.

"Was a man who tried it. His name was Calvin Raiford. Oh, he was an outlaw, sure enough, but Cal didn't like killin' none. Claimed it made him sick in body and mind. Nate Bonstall said it didn't used to, that Cal was a killer same as the rest of 'em, but he'd caught a bad case of the conscience somewhere along the road and it ruined his outlawin'. Alice, there, was sweet on Cal, weren't you, sis?"

"I don't want to talk about it," said Alice. She hung her dulcimer up on the wall and left the room. Sally hunched forward in her chair to listen to her father.

"Well, that was the truth of it. Cal, he went on raids with Skaggs an' his bunch, but he got sweet on Alice and said he'd help her and us get out. I knew it wouldn't come to nothing, but Alice and Sally thought Cal was their damned savior. They put stock in him when he said he'd get us all out."

Anders paused, took another swig from his glass of whiskey. He tweaked his nose without pulling on his earlobes.

"What happened?" asked Slocum.

"Cal and the bunch come in after a raid and I guess there was some killin' of innocent victims, 'cause Cal got drunk and told Skaggs he was going to light a shuck out of Pipestone. He never gave a thought to me and the gals, but got on his horse and started riding out of town like he had fire in his britches. All the boys stood outside the saloon and watched him ride almost clear to the end of the street. Then they all pulled their pistols and shot Cal in the back. He stayed in the saddle a long time, it seemed, but he went down, finally, and I counted eighteen bullet holes in him before I give up. Skaggs and his boys just stood there and laughed. It was great sport for them."

"I saw it happen," said Sally softly. "It was horrible."

Slocum looked at her face and felt an involuntary shudder course down his spine. It was not good for a young woman to see things like that. Seeing a man die was hard enough, but seeing him shot in the back and bleeding was something she would likely never forget.

"So, Slocum, maybe you better git while the gittin's good," said Pete. "You got a headstart. You might slip away in the dark and they won't find you. It's gonna rain tomorry, I reckon. Wind's comin' up and I saw mare's tails in the sky today. Some clouds building in the north, all right. Rain'll wash out your tracks."

Slocum knew Anders was right. He heard the wind now, sniffing at the cracks of the cabins, and he'd seen the wisps of high clouds curved like the tails of horses running in the wind. It could well rain tonight or tomorrow and he'd probably never get a better opportunity to clear out of Pipestone and go on his way. But there was something about this family and the others he had met, like Melanie, that made him want to stay and try to help. He might make things worse, but he had to take that chance. If he left now, he'd always have that nagging doubt, and he wouldn't like himself very much.

"I'm not going," said Slocum. "Not that way. I'll stay around, see what I can do." He rose from his chair, started to reach for his hat.

"You can stay the night," said Anders, smiling. "No use you goin' into town tonight. Might be trouble if you showed up now. Skaggs will be in an ugly mood. Let him sleep on it."

"You got room for me? I can throw a blanket on the floor here, or bunk out in the shed."

"You can have my bed," said Anders. "I wasn't gonna sleep much anyways."

"I wouldn't want to take your bed," said Slocum.

"Pa sleeps in his chair a lot," said Sally sheepishly. Anders did not admonish her. Instead, he finished off the whiskey in his glass, poured himself another drink. Slocum knew he was looking at a deeply troubled man. Pete had some demons to deal with and he was drinking to keep them away.

"You go on, Slocum," said Anders, waving his hand in front of him. "Sally will turn the bed down for you, won't you, honey?"

"Yes, Pa," said Sally, and batted her eyes at Slocum.

Sally turned down the coverlet on her father's bed, fluffed the simple pillows, smoothed the bedsheets with the flat of her hands. Slocum watched her, saw how the lamplight got tangled in her hair, made it look soft and shiny. She turned to him, spoke breathlessly.

"I hope you sleep well," she said quietly.

"I reckon I will," said Slocum.

"Well, good night to you, then."

"Good night, Sally."

She left the room and her scent lingered in the close air. He heard the door shut and let out a sigh as he sat down on the edge of the bed. The sheets were crisp and clean, smelled faintly of lye soap and the warming heat of the sun. They smelled of a woman's warm touch, and showed the care of a woman, too.

Slocum tugged off his boots, stripped down to his long johns, hanging his shirt, trousers, and gunbelt on the post nearest his head. He lay atop the coverlet and sheets, reached over, and turned down the lamp on the bedside table. The walls of the room drowned in the sudden darkness. Slocum closed his eyes, listened to the murmur of conversation drifting down the hall, leaking through the door.

The sound of voices soothed him, and his full belly, the liquor, weighted his drowsiness so that he drifted from consciousness, sank into slumber like a water-soaked log sinking in a dark sea. Soon the voices faded and Slocum slept, deaf to the ticking of the house as it settled in the quiet of night.

Soon, only the soft snoring of Pete Anders could be heard coming from the front room, and a barred owl hooted somewhere up on the ridge.

Slocum dreamed he was in a large hotel in some big Eastern city. Men in suits smiled at him, ushered him to the counter where the desk clerk demanded his papers. He handed them over, watched as the clerk stamped them, returned them. The clerk said he could visit the hotel, and the smiling men escorted the dreamer into the labyrinth, up wide stairs into rooms where wax figures stood frozen in position. The hotel was like a museum and one of the smiling men explained that this was where the town had been founded. Slocum tried to explain that one of the men had a rope around his neck, but no one would listen to him. The small group entered other rooms and one of them was a jail where Slocum was thrown into irons and taunted by a host of visitors. He struggled with his bonds and the smiling men began to laugh loudly, teasing him, pointing accusing fingers at him. Pretty girls came close to him and taunted him with their flesh, the flash of thighs. The dream took on the aspects of a nightmare as wild dogs came at him, leaping out of the darkness for his throat. Slocum struggled to bring up his arms, to fight them off, but his wrists were shackled. The women rubbed against him and the dogs snarled.

"John, John, what's the matter?" called a soft voice, and Slocum swam through the oceans of sleep, unshackled at last, and the walls of the hotel fell away like slats from a barrel when the rings are removed.

He opened his eyes, still drugged from sleep, addled by the dream and saw the shadowy face before his own.

"Sally?" he said.

A woman's laugh echoed hollow in the room. Slocum felt a hand caress his chest, saw the shadowed face come close. He felt a woman's lips brush against his cheek. A tingle of electricity charged his spine.

"Sally?" he asked again.

The woman's hand slid around his side, scurried up his back and he felt fingers run gently through his hair. Her lips glided across his and he jolted out of his sleepy stupor as he felt the heat and softness, the delicate feather touch of her mouth on his.

"Don't you think Sally is a little young for you?"

"Alice?"

"Yes," she crooned, "Alice, and I'm shocked that you thought it would be my niece."

"Alice," he breathed, blinking his eyes in the darkness, startled by the revelation. He had seen Sally last, and he had thought it would have been she who came to him in the dark of night. "Yeah, sure. Alice."

"Are you disappointed?"

"No." He let out a breath and she pulled him close to her, nudged her face against his. He put his arms around her, and there was silk on her shoulders, or satin, a smooth surface that excited him. He kissed her, touched a breast with his hand as he fumbled at her garment, a robe, he guessed, and the tactile sensation made his flesh crinkle.

She was naked under the robe and her skin was hot. Slocum drew her to him, slipped the robe from her shoulders, touched the tips of her taut nipples. He felt Alice shudder in his arms and her hand dove inside his long johns and grasped his manhood, squeezed it gently. He was hard and she knew it now, knew she had only to wait a little while to claim his manhood, to pull it inside her until it was part of her.

"I want you," she breathed in his ear.

"I want you, too," he rasped. She tugged at his long johns, drew them down his legs. He peeled off her robe and they clung to each other for a moment until he lay her gently on her back. She touched his stalk again and the fire in her touch shot through him, made his cock throb, made his pulse drum there and in his temples.

She spread her legs and Slocum mounted her, eased into her until she buckled, arched her back, and cried out with the pleasure of it. He burrowed deep and she thrashed as the orgasm possessed her.

"Yes, yes," she screamed softly and Slocum stroked

her, in and out, until she shook with spasms.

"I'm glad you came to my bed," husked Slocum.

"I knew I would from the moment I first laid eyes on you," she whispered, her voice quavery with excitement. "I never wanted a man so bad."

When he made her buck again, he knew it was so.

9

The town was quiet when Slocum stole back to the hotel and tiptoed up to his room. Melanie Lovelace was sound asleep on his bed, curled up like a kitten. In repose, she looked like a child taking a nap. He shook her gently, saw her eyes widen in surprise.

"John—I—I was worried about you. Pa, he got drunk last night, said Skaggs was going to kill you."

"Well, now, I wouldn't worry about that. Skaggs has no reason to kill me."

"But Pa said you ran off and Skaggs would hunt you down."

"I'm here, aren't I?"

She sat up, rubbed sleep from her eyes. She looked out the window, saw the sky beginning to lighten.

"Oh, what time is it? I've got to get home before Pa wakes up."

"About six o'clock, I reckon. How come you came here? How did you get in?"

"I've got a key that unlocks all the doors. I sometimes clean the rooms here. I came to wait for you. I knew you'd come back. Where've you been?"

"Oh, I just wanted to be by myself," he lied. "Those chaperones were getting on my nerves."

Melanie laughed. She hopped off the bed, straightened her skirt. She brushed her hair with her hands, stood on tiptoe and gave Slocum a kiss.

"I wish you'd come back earlier," she pouted.

"Me too," he grinned.

In a moment, she was gone, and Slocum poured water from the pitcher into a basin, dashed some on his face. He shaved, taking his time, thinking. Skaggs was probably in a bad mood, but he'd get over it. Jack Lovelace had a big mouth and drank too much. He didn't want any trouble with him. But he was prepared to fight if it came to that. He hoped it did not, for Melanie's sake. She had told him to be careful before she left, and he saw the questioning in her eyes. Somehow, he had to help her escape, along with the others, and he had no hankering to stay around Pipe-stone himself any longer than was necessary.

A plan began to form in Slocum's mind as he scraped his beard down to the skin with a straight razor he kept among his necessaries in his saddlebag. Part of his plan would mean doing some things in secret, the first of which would be to begin moving his personal possessions from the hotel to a hiding place in the timber.

He knew he would only be able to do this at night. None of Skaggs's men would fall for the same trick twice. Even that would be difficult, for he was sure that Skaggs would demand an increase in vigilance from now on.

Slocum finished shaving, wiped his face clean of lather,

changed his shirt. He checked his pistols, the .31 Colts, replaced one of the percussion caps. From now on, he would have to have his wits about him even more than before. When he was finished, he left the room, walked down the stairs and through the lobby, into the small dining room. The place was empty, but he heard pots clanging in the kitchen. He walked through the swinging doors into the kitchen. A man bent over the woodstove, stoking the firebox.

"Won't be no food nor coffee for a half hour yet," said the man, a grizzled, balding man in a grimy apron.

"O.K.," said Slocum, "but I could eat the south end of a northbound horse."

"Well, I'm plumb out of horse, but we got some beef. Gonna be ten or twelve in for breakfast purty quick and I reckon you're the reason if you be Slocum."

"I am."

"Name's Jellico. Tom Jellico. Emmett's got a dozen riders out lookin' for you, mister, and I'm supposed to tell Lou, the desk clerk, if I see hide er hair of you."

"I'll tell him myself," said Slocum amiably. "There was no one at the desk when I came down."

"You were up in your room?"

"Sure was. All night. Slept like a babe."

Slocum grinned and walked out of the kitchen.

"Well, I'll be damned," said Jellico, and Slocum heard the iron lid of the firebox slam down hard.

When Slocum returned to the lobby, Lou was stretching and yawning. He looked up, startled, as Slocum came up to the desk.

"Any messages?" Slocum asked.

"Where you been, Slocum?"

"Like I told Jellico, upstairs sleeping. You got good tick in that mattress."

"I checked your room last night about ten and you weren't in there."

"Must have gone out to piss," said Slocum, smiling. "Anyway, you can tell Skaggs I'm gonna have coffee and vittles."

Slocum touched a finger to his hat and left Lou with his mouth hanging open. He returned to the dining room and sat at a table, waited. Ten minutes later, Jellico brought a pot of coffee and a cup out and set them down. He poured the cup full. The aroma drifted to Slocum's nostrils on clouds of steam.

"Thanks," he said.

"I got beefsteak and taters, no eggs."

"I'll take what you got," said Slocum.

"Mister, I sure hope Emmett's in a good mood this mornin'. He was plumb belchin' fire last night."

"What happened?"

"They run into some trouble rustlin' beef and Emmett thinks they was follered here. Just 'fore they got back to Pipestone, they seen a rider climb a ridge and then light out. Emmett's mighty nervous."

"Don't blame him a bit," said Slocum. "I hear they hang cattle rustlers sames as horsethieves."

Jellico's face went dark and he scurried away, muttering to himself. Slocum chuckled and picked up his coffee cup, blew on it before he touched it to his lips. The coffee was scalding hot, but he got enough in him to know that his stomach was thinking his throat was cut.

He heard the sound of hoofbeats on the street outside. Shadows passed the windows and there was the sound of scuffling hooves as the men reined up their mounts. Men came into the cafe from the street, bypassing the lobby of the hotel, their boots clumping on the rough hardwood flooring. Heading the pack was Nate Bonstall. Right behind came Rufus Harding. Slocum didn't know the others, but he had a pretty good idea that none of them would hesitate to put a bullet in his back.

"Slocum," drawled Bonstall, "where in hell have you been? We been looking high and low for you."

"I've been drawing shuteye time up in my room," Slocum said evenly.

"The hell you say," blurted Harding, taking off his hat and slapping it against his thigh.

"Didn't hear anyone knock on my door," said Slocum.

The men looked at one another, foolish-eyed, and Slocum suppressed a laugh. One of them left and Slocum figured he was going after Skaggs. Harding and Bonstall sat down at his table. Both men stared at Slocum for a long time before they broke into wide grins.

"Don't you beat all, though," said Bonstall. "Slocum, you do keep a man on edge. Here we been riding all over a-huntin' you and you here all the time, sleepin' like a babe."

"Else you turned invisible," said Harding, not so sure that he wasn't being gulled. "Nate, whyn't you get us some coffee. I reckon Emmett will be along shortly and want to jaw with our friend here."

Bonstall went after coffee and Slocum sipped his. The cook brought his breakfast just as Emmett Skaggs entered the cafe, followed by the man who had gone to fetch him. Skaggs waved the hardcase to a table, stalked over to throw his shadow over Slocum.

"You and me got to talk. Rufus, you find another place to light."

Harding got up and Skaggs took his chair. Bonstall set a full coffee cup in front of him. Skaggs ignored it while he stared at Slocum, sizing him up, staring into his green eyes as if trying to make him flinch.

Slocum held his gaze steady. His face bore no expression. He ate his breakfast while Skaggs looked on.

"Slocum," said Skaggs, "I just don't rightly know what to make of you. I think we got to get some things straight, though, right here and now."

"Suit yourself, Skaggs."

"I been a long time gettin' this town together. We first come here and camped on bare ground. Then we brung in tents and it made a pretty good hideout. Then me and the boys talked about puttin' up a permanent town, one where we could feel to home and not worry about law and such. We put some pretty good money into Pipestone and we kept it a secret. That was the first thing we agreed on—nobody outside the bunch could know where we was. We had some law track us here and they was mighty sorry. Now, I don't think you're law, you keep lookin' over your own shoulder too damn much, but you got to realize why you got to stay. You get out and talk about what you seen here and next thing you know they's going to be marshals and sheriffs pourin' in here like locusts."

"You can't keep a secret this big very long," said Slocum quietly. "Even if I kept my mouth shut."

"Meanin'?"

"Meaning people aren't stupid. You've been robbing folks and running off to hide somewhere. Pretty soon, somebody smart's going to narrow it down, find their way here."

Skaggs frowned. His eyes knotted up into slits.

"I think we got company comin', in fact," admitted Skaggs. "Maybe today, maybe tomorry."

"Well, that's what I mean."

"Yeah, we had some trouble this time out," said Skaggs. "We got shot up pretty bad and I heard one of the men threaten us when he rode off, sayin' the vigilantes would be on our trail."

"Vigilantes?" Slocum didn't like the sound of the word.

"That's what he said, and I hope to hell he was just a-braggin' on an empty gun. I just don't rightly know."

"So, can you be tracked here?"

"Maybe," said Skaggs. "Just maybe we was follered in here this time. Boys said they saw tracks and we saw a rider on the ridge light out when he seen we saw him."

"Well, you got troubles, then," said Slocum, "and it doesn't make any difference whether I'm here or not."

"That ain't the point. If you ain't for us, you're agin' us, and I want to know which way it's gonna be."

Slocum chewed on a chunk of beefsteak, shifted it to the other side of his mouth. He looked at Skaggs squarely, his face impassive.

"I walked in here by accident, Skaggs," said Slocum. "That was my bad luck. And now you want me to stay. Maybe that's yours."

Skaggs laughed.

"Slocum, you ain't a man to back down. I like that. You could put some money in your pockets riding for me. We got a good thing here. We split even, and ten percent goes back into the town. We got our own economy here. It's better'n some places I been."

"You're asking me to join you?"

"Either that or . . ." Skaggs shrugged, letting it hang.

"You have anybody leave you before?"

"Not that lived very long." There was a hard edge to Skaggs's voice when he said that. "Slocum, you could become a rich man. It's only a matter of time."

Slocum finished off his steak, washed it down with a swallow of coffee. He pushed back from the table, wiped his mouth with a napkin. He thought about Skaggs's offer.

At any other time or place he would have laughed in the man's face. What did a caged eagle need with money? he thought. What good would money be if you could only spend it one place? He still didn't know the kind of hold Skaggs held on his men, the others who lived in Pipestone, but it was a powerful hold, he knew. Fear, maybe. There was something not quite right about Skaggs. He lived in a world of his own making, but just as false as the fronts of the buildings in town. There was nothing behind him but greed and a lust for power. That was what made him dangerous, Slocum was sure.

"I'll think about it some," Slocum said. "You buy me a drink this evening and I'll give you my answer."

"It better be the right answer," said Skaggs, and there was no humor in his tone.

"I'd like to get on my horse, ride around," said Slocum, standing up.

"So long as you don't mind company," said Skaggs. "You made a couple of my men look pretty foolish yesterday."

"They crowded me."

"That's their job. And, by the way, the breakfast's on me. You're a guest of mine. Until tonight."

"You seem like a fair man, Skaggs," said Slocum, without a trace of underlying sarcasm. "Mighty obliged."

Slocum stalked from the room. Skaggs nodded to two men, who got up and followed Slocum out the door. Slocum looked back inside at Skaggs. Skaggs smiled, without a trace of humor on his lips.

Slocum now knew that his plan would not work. The two men who accompanied him to the stables were probably handpicked. They had the cold pale eyes of killers, and they walked two paces behind him, hands on their pistol butts.

"You got names?" Slocum asked amiably when they reached the stables.

"I'm Haskins, he's Tinker," said one of the men. They were in their early thirties, Slocum figured, with faces hard as boot leather, thin mouths, lips cracked by sun and weather, lean as whips.

"Thought we'd ride around some," Slocum said. "I don't want to go soft with all this good food and company."

"We'll ride around with you," said Jim Haskins. "You got an hour."

"Well, I won't get saddle sores, anyway," said Slocum. Neither man said a word.

Slocum saddled his horse, looked over the mounts of the two hardcases. Haskins threw a blanket on a black gelding, and Bill Tinker put a saddle on a sorrel. Both horses looked sure-footed and sleek, with good chests. Slocum rode ahead of the two men, northeast of town over a well-worn road. He knew that this was the direction the bunch took when they went out on raids. He wanted to see some of the country, see what he faced if he managed to escape.

They crossed the little creek that provided water for the town, rode between small rolling hills to a narrow valley. The mountains rose up on their left, craggy and stippled with trees. Slocum saw lion tracks and bear scat, a high pass further on, maybe an hour's ride. He gave his horse his head, turned him when they had ridden a half hour.

"Seen enough?" asked Haskins.

"Fine country," said Slocum.

"We like it."

Slocum could see that he wasn't going to make any

friends here. As he turned his horse, he saw a flash of light off toward the mountain pass. The others missed it. He said nothing. Could be Crow, he thought, but an answering flash across the cut made him wonder.

Now, with his back to the high peaks, Slocum headed back to town. He looked back only once, and saw no flashes, but he knew there were men in the mountans, red or white, and they were watching the high pass.

There was another bunk in Slocum's room when he returned, and a man in it. Haskins and Tinker stayed outside as he went in. The man on the bunk sat up, grinned. He held a sawed-off, double-barreled shotgun in his hands. He looked to be in his mid-twenties, with tousled light hair, close-set hazel eyes that were as vacant as olive pits.

"Name's Jethro Caudill," he said. "Emmett thought you might want some company."

"Meaning you or that Greener you got in your hands?"

"Oh, this here scattergun's for daylight," grinned Jethro.

"Daylight?"

"Yeah, it lets daylight in when somebody I don't like blocks my way. Like, you know, when I say 'shut up,' and a feller thinks I said 'stand up'?"

"Yeah, I get the point."

"That's jes' fine, Mr. Slocum. I wouldn't want no mis-understandin'."

Slocum lay on the bed, crossed his legs, and folded his arms up behind his head. Jethro sat there, grinning idiotically, the front brim of his hat pushed back flat, his hair sticking out like straw from underneath. Slocum closed his eyes, quelling the anger rising in him. Skaggs was making it hard, every bit of it. Next he'd put bars on the windows, a padlock on the door.

"Boy, we had us a time, yestiddy," said Caudill. "Bullets a-flyin', smoke ever'wheres. I got me a old boy with my Greener. I call this scattergun Snake Charmer, you know. It kills snakes real good. Near cut that feller in two, it did."

Slocum opened his eyes, glared at Jethro coldly.

"Your job call for torture, too?" Slocum asked.

"Huh?"

"You're supposed to guard me, I reckon, Caudill, not bore me to death with your gabbing."

Caudill blinked, pouted. He drew back, affronted.

"Now, you ain't got no cause to insult me, Mr. Slocum. I was just trying to strike up a friendly conversation."

Slocum sat up, slid off the bed. He walked over to Caudill, so close that the young man would have to draw to one side to use his shotgun.

"Now, you listen to me, sonny," said Slocum. "Anytime I want a bunkmate, I'll ask for one. You take your snake charmer and get out of here. Tell Skaggs I'll see him tonight, as promised."

"You ain't . . ." Caudill tried to bring the Greener down. Slocum grabbed the twin barrels and wrenched the weapon from Caudill's hands. Then he drove a straight right into Jethro's forehead, smashing him into the wall. His head made a loud thump as it struck the wood. Slocum grabbed Jethro by the collar and jerked him upright.

He dragged him to the door, opened it, and threw Jethro out into the hall. In the hall, Tinker started to go for his pistol.

Slocum brought the Greener down level, cocked it.

"Just pull it a little ways, Tinker," said Slocum, "and I'll blow your guts all over this hotel."

Tinker froze.

"What's goin' on here?" asked Tinker, and Slocum saw that he was alone.

"I don't like Jethro's company is all," said Slocum. "Get him out of here."

Slocum backed off, closed the door. He heard the murmur of voices, the high-pitched hysteria in Jethro's. Tinker evidently calmed the young man down, because he heard boots ring on the floor a few moments later and then it was quiet. Slocum lay down on the cot and listened, but heard nothing. Every so often, he heard Tinker shift his weight. After a while another man came up and relieved him at guard. But no one tried to enter his room.

Slocum kept the Greener cocked, aimed at the door.

There was nothing to do but wait for the nightfall.

It was going to be a long day.

10

The sun hung over the Big Horn mountains a long time that summer eve. Long before it set, the Pipestone Saloon was crowded, and men came in to take supper and drink hard drinks to forget their troubles. Skaggs took up a table there, and watched the windows change colors, watched the bars of light turn from silken wheat to gold and then to soft diffused shades of pale goldenrod and amber.

He fisted a handful of glass brimmed with whiskey and stared at the windows, watched the light change and shift like stream waters under clouds. The light fascinated him because it was hypnotic. It took him away from where he was sitting, and made him think of other times, of boyhood days and afternoons on the trail. He had slept that afternoon and felt fresh and alive, but there was a tugging at his brain, like a fishhook that pulled at memory. He did not want to go back to those times, but they were always there, in his mind, and they came up suddenly when he looked through windows with a glass in his hand,

The rock and the hogs. That's what he remembered about being a boy. His pa and he cleared the land in Fairview, Arkansas, along Osage Creek. They built a rock boat and it was Emmett's job to dig out the rocks and fill it up, hitch the mule, Pete, to the boat and haul the rocks away, stack them into a fence. His back hurt every time he thought about those rocks, and after every rain there would be more of them and he began to think that Arkansas land grew rocks just like it grew potatoes and corn and squash.

The goddamned hogs, too. His pa got the idea to raise pigs and he bought Poland Chinas and Hampshire Reds and penned 'em up. Emmett had to slop 'em every morning, put straw in their stalls, clean it out when it turned to mud and shit. He could still smell the hogs, especially at butchering time, the time he dreaded most of all. Men would come from all the farms and help slaughter the hogs and they'd light fires under the big kettles full of water. They'd gut out the hogs and the stench was unbearable. They hung the dead hogs from the trees and then scalded all the hairs off in the boiling water. The soggy smell of hog hair and the reek of guts still lingered in his nostrils every time he thought of butchering day.

Emmett cleared his brain of thoughts and took a swig of whiskey. He looked away from the darkening window and sniffed the air in the saloon. Cigar and cigarette smoke washed out the memory of hog guts and scalded pigs hanging lifeless and huge from the big box elders his pa had planted before he was born.

But he couldn't erase the memory of the War so easily. Folks in his part of the country, those who lived along the Arkansas–Missouri border, were caught in the struggle between North and South, with some sympathetic to the

Union, others secesh. Everybody was suspicious of everybody else and the Union troops combing the countryside
and shooting anyone who looked like a rebel. The Skaggs
family was caught there, like rats in a well. Emmett's pa
had been shot down by Confederates and that's what made
it hard for Emmett. He wanted to fight with the boys in
gray, but they had killed his pa, so he ended up with a
bunch of ragtaggle outlaws who stole from both sides of
the border.

He came back after the war to burned-out towns, rubble, dead kin, and looked at the rocks and the empty hog
pens and just rode on out west, away from his broken-
hearted ma, and never looked back, not once. He didn't
know if she was alive or not. He didn't care. She had
turned into an old woman because of the War, with vacant
eyes and a palsy he couldn't bear to watch. That's how he
remembered his ma. Her hair gray and stringy and that
empty look in her eyes. The shaking in her hands. The
farm was taken over for taxes and grown up with weeds
and black locust. It made him sick to think of it, because
despite the pain he had endured, he and his pa had left their
blood on the land and it had all been taken away.

He had been doing the same thing ever since. Taking
away. Getting back at the Union and the Seceshes for what
they did to his ma and pa, to their farm. And now he had
built a town and it was his town and he liked the smell of
fresh-sawed lumber, the aroma of pine sawdust and new-
ness about it. Pipestone stood over the ashes of Fairview,
burned to the ground by troops of both sides, only the
stone chimneys left standing like tall tombstones over the
charred remains of the town where he'd grown up so long
ago.

"Emmett, he's comin'," said Nate Wales.

"Huh?" asked Skaggs, jerked from his reverie by the sound of Wales's voice.

"Slocum. He's headin' for the saloon."

"Yeah, good. We'll see what that son of a bitch has to say."

He looked toward the door, heard it creak on its leather hinges as Slocum pushed through it. His frame filled the doorway for a minute. Skaggs saw the Greener in his hands, saw that it was broken. Slocum strode toward him, stopped at his table, dropped the shotgun on the surface. Behind Slocum, Harding and Bonstall, his guards, took up positions that flanked the doorway.

"Next time, Skaggs," said Slocum, "don't give a kid a man's toy."

"Jethro feels pretty bad about that."

"He's liable to blow his head off if he's not careful."

"Or yours, Slocum."

Slocum said nothing. Skaggs motioned to a chair.

"Set and have a drink, Slocum."

Slocum sat down.

"Hungry?"

"I ate at the hotel, told Cookie to charge it to you."

Skaggs threw his head back and laughed.

"You got a sense of humor anyways, Slocum. I like that in a man."

Skaggs snapped his fingers and the barkeep brought another glass. Skaggs poured whiskey for both of them, lifted his glass in a toast.

"Well, I'm wondering what to celebrate," said Skaggs. "Your funeral or your welcome into my bunch."

"Maybe both," said Slocum, "but I'll ride with you if you deal fair."

"Good!" exclaimed Skaggs. "Welcome, Slocum."

The two men touched glasses and drank. The others in

the saloon noted the incident and all raised their glasses. Bonstall and Harding shifted their feet and looked at one another.

"Next raid we go on," said Skaggs, "you'll ride at my side. I'm sending scouts out tomorrow. We should have something to go on in a few days."

"That's good. I don't like being cooped up."

"You prove yourself, Slocum, and you'll have free run, same as any of the others I ride with."

Slocum finished his drink, stood up.

"I'll be getting some shuteye, Skaggs."

"Call me Emmett."

"Emmett, good night."

Skaggs nodded to Bonstall and Harding as Slocum left the saloon. They followed him, but at a greater distance than before. At the hotel, Harding stayed outside. Bonstall went upstairs with Slocum.

"Good night, Slocum," he said. "Glad you decided to join us."

"I hope it works out," said Slocum. "Good night, Nate."

Nate Bonstall grinned.

Slocum slept deep, dreamed little. He was up at the crack of dawn, edgy for some reason. He dressed quickly, looked out the window, down onto the street. Everything seemed quiet and normal. He strapped on his gunbelt, checked the cylinders of both Colts. He checked the spare cylinders, saw that they were fully loaded.

He opened the door of his room, looked out into the hall. It was empty. No guard. It was just too damned quiet.

Slocum went down into the lobby. It was deserted. There was no one in the dining room or the kitchen. He went back to the lobby, stood there, looking out the window. He looked up and down the street. Then he saw slight movement from across the street. Between two buildings a man stood, holding a rifle loosely across his chest. Slocum looked up, saw the top of a man's hat. The man moved and he saw part of his face. He was crouched behind a false front, peering north.

Slocum saw a man skulking behind the water trough in front of the stables, and a window curtain fluttered in another building. Slocum barely saw the outline of an armed man, the barrel of a rifle poking through the open window.

As the light gradually grew stronger, Slocum heard a distant shout. Then came a gunshot from the south end of town. Another rifle boomed at the north end. The man in the window leaned out and shouted.

"Here they come!"

"Here come the Vigilantes!" yelled the man behind the false front.

Slocum eased the door open, stood shielded by the wall, ready to run out if the opportunity presented itself. He did not have long to wait. Hoofbeats sounded on the street, and the firing became more rapid. Riders came from both directions. Glass windows popped and shattered as stray rifle and pistol fire whipped bullets in every direction. The man behind the watering trough stood up, staggered, and fell. Smoke filled the street. The hotel window pane blew inwards as a heavy-caliber rifle bullet smashed the glass. Slocum ducked as glass showered over his shoulders.

Riders rode in from both directions, firing from their saddles. Horses screamed and the shouts of men drifted through the thick clouds of white smoke. A rider clutched his chest and slid over the cantle, twisted in the air, hit the ground headfirst. The horse reared and began to kick and buck as bullets whistled around it. Slocum saw a man step out of a store with a sawed-off Greener in his hands. He took aim at a Vigilante, let him have both barrels at close range. The man's face disappeared in a cloud of blood and he shot out of the saddle as the second charge caught him in the chest. His horse skidded to a halt, pranced off, reins trailing in the dust.

Now, men were screaming as they went down in a hail of outlaw bullets. Slocum realized that the Vigilantes were trapped, the town sealed off, with outlaws closing the pincers from both directions. A man and his horse crashed through the building across the street from the hotel, his back riddled with bullets, blood streaming down his tattered shirt, staining his saddle.

Slocum stepped outside the hotel, drew one of his pistols. He could barely see through the smoke, but he saw a young boy ride up, turn his horse, and dive off as bullets fried the air around him. A man stepped out, brained the lad with his rifle butt, then shot him in cold blood at close range. Slocum couldn't see who the outlaw was, but he drew a bead with his Colt and shot him in the side. He fired again as the man staggered toward him, saw him go down with a bullet hole in the middle of his face. Slocum caught up a loose horse, swung up into the saddle.

He rode through the firestorm, hugging the side of the lean black horse with the quartercircle N brand burned into its hip, saw the pack of Vigilantes trapped at the north end of town. He rode toward them, his hat brim pulled down low, and fired his pistol at the smoke-puffs on the buildings, at the orange flashes in doorways.

"This way," Slocum shouted. "You've got no chance there."

One of the men in the center of the pack saw him, shouted to the others. He rallied them to follow the lone horseman toward the south of town. Shooting their way clear, they raced after Slocum, who was spearheading their escape through the smoke.

Slocum shot at men on both sides of the street, made them duck for cover. Behind him, a dozen men or more thundered after him, firing, too, and his nostrils burned with the acrid stench of black powder. Pipestone outlaws on horseback tried to block his way, but he shot through them like a greased pig, saw them fall away, abandon their mounts, and run for cover like gray squirrels before the eagle's shadow.

He cleared the edge of town, looked back to see the Vigilantes appear out of the thick smoke like horsemen from Hell. He gestured to his right, turned his captured mount, headed for the hills, the sheltering timber. The men came after him and as he climbed the ridge, he saw that Skaggs and his men had taken up their horses, were following, shooting on the run.

Bullets whistled harmlessly through the trees, or whanged off rocks with careening whines. Slocum found a game trail, circled above the town, headed for the pass. He reloaded his pistols, one by one, pulling the cylinders, popping in fresh ones. His Navy Colts barked as he covered the fleeing men behind him, allowed them the chance to reload. Soon, they were in a bunch, and riding for the pass.

Slocum rode ahead of the Vigilantes once again, turned and held up his hand in a gesture meant to halt them. The riders swarmed around him as he reined up, kicking up dust. The firing behind them had stopped a good five minutes before and now it was quiet. But in the distance, below them, they heard the thunk of iron shoes on the road leading out of the valley. With a sinking sensation, Slocum knew that Skaggs was a better general than he had thought. The Pipestone outlaws were heading for the pass, as sure as it was day and the sun already rising over the plains to kiss the peaks of the mountains.

Slocum holstered his Colts and as soon as they were in leather, one of the Vigilantes, a red-faced, heavy-set man on a tall bay mare, threw down on him.

"Mister, tell me one good reason why I shouldn't shoot you out of the saddle right here and now."

"If I hadn't gotten you out of there, you and the other men would be lying dead in the street."

"He's one of 'em, I tell ya," said a young man, who looked remarkably like the boy Slocum had seen killed. "He's playin' a damned trick on us."

Slocum looked at the man with the .44 caliber Remington in his hand and at the others. They looked to be ranchers, their faces raw from wind and weather, their tight mouths, their double-cinched saddles and coiled lariats. He looked at each man in turn and saw the hatred in their eyes.

"He's a-ridin' Billy's horse," said an older man. "Lou, you better shoot him quick or shake out some hemp."

"Where'd you get that horse, stranger?" asked the man who had been called Lou.

"Caught him up, so I could get you and me out of there. Skaggs and his men were waiting for you. You didn't have a chance."

"See, was I right, Lou? Emmett Skaggs. Had a damned hunch." The speaker was a man in his mid-thirties, slow-drawled voice with a slight rasp to it, whip-lean and, from the looks of him, more at home on a horse than on foot. "This is one of his bunch, sure as hell, and I say put his lamp out."

"Yeah, Lou, we got dead back there. Billy, I think, and Jess, four or five others I don't see here."

"You know what I think?" asked Lou. "I think this feller

was sent to slow us down so the rest of the bunch can pick us off. We were doing all right."

"No," said Slocum. "He had you where he wanted you. There were men lined up all along that street and he had you blocked both ways."

"Who in hell are you?" asked Lou.

"The name's Slocum. John Slocum. I was being held prisoner by Skaggs."

"A likely story," said Lou.

"Well, are you going to shoot him or jaw with him all day?" asked one of the Vigilante ranchers.

"Slocum, I'm Lou Norman," said the leader. "I run a ranch down Cheyenne way. Me and my men lost a herd a year ago, driving up to the Gallatin Valley. This time, we come prepared, and we joined up with Vigilantes out of Bannock and Virginny City. We got a herd scattered from hell to breakfast, but we'll get 'em back. We shot some men up pretty bad, but the main bunch got clean away. We been trackin' this bunch for three days and I'm pretty sure I saw you ridin' with two of 'em yesterday."

"I saw your mirror-signals in the hills yesterday, that's true, but those two men had guns on me. I tell you, I've been a prisoner here."

"What the hell town is this anyway?" asked one of the Vigilantes. "I never heard of it before."

"Skaggs calls it Pipestone. It's an outlaw town."

"Seems to me you know a lot about it. Skaggs do you a dirty deal, Slocum?"

"No, I walked in here by mistake, after a run-in with Crow who stole my horse. After that, Skaggs wouldn't let me go. I got my horse back, but I lost my freedom."

Some of the men guffawed. It was plain to Slocum that few, if any, believed him. One thing was for sure. Norman didn't believe him.

"Paxton, you and Jerry Scrimsher go on the scout. Find out where that bunch is headed, and check our back trail. We'll wait for you here. Joe, you and Dobbs ride a big circle and tell me what you see." Norman gave the orders and the men didn't hesitate to carry them out. Slocum watched the four men ride off. He knew exactly where Skaggs was headed—for the pass.

"Slocum," said Norman, "far as I can see, there's only one way into this valley. Over that pass, right?"

"It doesn't make any difference. Skaggs will have men waiting for you whichever way you go. But that's the only way I know of at the moment. I think that's why he picked this place to build a hideout."

"Lou, I say we get blood for blood. This feller's one of 'em. I seen him yesterday through the glass, plain as I'm lookin' at him now. He warn't no prisoner. Him and those other two were scoutin'."

"Yeah, I agree with Tom," said another man. "I seen 'em, too."

"Shoot him now and be done with it," said Tom Peppering.

"Hang him," said the other man.

"We'll wait until the others get back and take a vote," said Norman. "You boys roll some smokes and cool down."

The men rolled quirlies and Norman gave one to Slocum, already lit. Some of the men rubbed down their horses, tightened their cinches. Slocum drew the smoke into his lungs, wondering if it would be his last cigarette on this earth. Norman kept looking at him, and kept the pistol trained on him.

They all jumped when they heard the sound of gunfire in the distance. A few moments later, Jerry Scrimsher came riding in, his horse lathered.

"They shot Dick Paxton," he panted. "They're all over the road, like fleas."

"Christ," said Norman. His eyes narrowed to slits as he looked at Slocum.

Kevin Dobbs and Joe Parnell came riding in from different directions.

"See anything?" asked Lou Norman.

"They're up in the pass, and along the road," said Dobbs. "I heard 'em talkin' about Slocum here."

"What'd they say?" asked Norman.

"Said they hoped he come back with some Vigilante scalps," said Dobbs.

"You're a goddamned liar," said Slocum.

"Joe, shake out a rope," said Norman coldly.

11

Slocum watched as Parnell made a thick hangman's knot in the rope, tied a loop. Scrimsher rode up and pulled the Navy Colts from his holsters. Dobbs tied Slocum's hands behind his back. One of the others rode off a little ways, came back in a few moments.

"There's a big old juniper over there," he said. "It'll hold him long enough to break his neck."

Slocum shuddered.

Norman grabbed the black's reins, led off. The others fell into formation on both sides of him, their faces grim, etched with hard lines of anger. Slocum heard the raucous protest of a jay and saw a crow fly over, chased by a pair of blackbirds. Deer flies boiled up from the grasses and flocked in gray clumps on man and horse alike. He felt their needlelike stings in his sweat-soaked back and on his legs where they came out of his boots.

No one said a word until they came to the juniper. Parnell threw the lean end of the rope over a jutting limb and caught it as it fell back over. He threw it over again and tested for the slippage. Norman led Slocum under the tree. Scrimsher put the loop around Slocum's neck, pulled the knot up tight under his ear. He nodded to Parnell, who started taking out slack.

Slocum looked up at the sky. It had never seemed so blue before. The sights and sounds, the images of the men around him, stood out in vivid relief. He felt the blood pound in his temples, felt his heartbeat strong and fast. He looked at the faces of the men gathered around him, their hands on their pommels or saddlehorns, hunched forward.

"Any last words, Slocum?" asked Norman.

"A few."

"Make it short. We don't have time for long speeches."

"You men are riled," said Slocum. "I don't blame you for getting damned good and mad. But you're so mad, you want revenge on somebody, anybody, and you picked me. But I'm not your enemy. And, if you kill me, you're making sure that Skaggs's other victims will probably die as well. I was trying to get Pete Anders, his daughter Sally, and his sister, Alice, out of Pipestone. I had a plan and you boys came riding in, shooting off your guns and I got caught in the middle."

"Hey, wait a minute!" shouted Parnell. "You're sayin' Pete Anders is a prisoner in that town?"

"Just as sure as I was," said Slocum.

"Hell, we wondered what happened to Pete," said Scrimsher. "He just up and disappeared one day."

"There's other folks in there wanting to get out, too," said Slocum. "They were depending on me. As you already might have guessed, Skaggs doesn't let anyone in or out without his say-so."

"By gum, I believe he's right," said Dobbs. "I knowed

Pete, too, and he'd never go along with Skaggs less'n he had a knife at his back."

"Slocum, I think we might have jumped to the wrong conclusion," said Norman. The others nodded. Parnell slipped the noose off Slocum's neck. Scrimsher untied Slocum's bonds and Norman saw to it that his pistols were returned. Slocum rubbed his neck, swallowed hard.

"We've got to take that town," said Norman. "You got any ideas?"

"No, you won't stand a chance there now. But, if I were you, I'd split up this bunch. Skaggs will take no chances on you or anyone else telling the law where Pipestone is. That's his stronghold and he's mighty proud of it. He'll be out in force, looking for every one of us. We've already been too long here. Skaggs isn't dumb. I reckon he's had some fighting time with guerrillas, and he knows this country."

"We know," said Norman wryly. "We've tried to track this jasper before. We did it, this time, but—"

"Don't look back," said Slocum. "We've got to get out of here, if we can, and get better organized. We may need more men before this is finished."

"All right, men," said Norman. "We split up. You're on your own. Try to make it through the pass after dark. We'll meet on the other side. You know the place."

The men all nodded. They rode off, leaving Lou Norman and Slocum alone.

"What about you?" asked Norman.

"We'll stick together. I did some guerrilla fighting myself. You?"

"I spent the War in a supply depot," admitted Norman. "I never got out of St. Louis."

"You were lucky, maybe," said Slocum. "Follow me."

Slocum rode to a low ridge, kept just below it, following the skyline. He let the horse walk, did not press it. Once in a while, he dismounted, walked to the ridge, and climbed a tree. There, he could view the pass, the slash it made through the mountains, and he could see some of the valley, too. He saw no men, Skaggs's or Norman's, but he hadn't expected to. He was looking for the glint of sun on a rifle barrel, movement, the sway of a tree branch, anything that would suggest where men might be hiding.

Once, they stopped to drink from Norman's canteen. That was when the rancher asked about the boy.

"Did you see Billy go down?"

"Was that the boy's name?"

"Yes."

"I saw him."

"Was it—was it quick?"

"He was executed. It was quick."

"Jesus," said Norman, and fought down a sob that rose in his throat.

"You knew him well?" asked Slocum quietly, after a moment.

"He was my kid brother."

"I'm sorry," said Slocum, and he thought of the brutal blow struck by the man who put a bullet in the boy's head. He thought about the man who did it, and, though it hadn't registered at the time, he knew without a doubt who the killer was. Nate Bonstall.

"We lost six men back there," said Norman. "There were nineteen of us going in. We lost two in the raid. We found one of theirs by a creek. Might have wounded a couple more."

"I think you bloodied Skaggs pretty bad," said Slocum.

"Not bad enough."

"No. But the winner hasn't been declared yet."

The two men rode on, hugging the skyline, staying to

the trees. Slocum avoided crossing any open spaces and sometimes their route took them lower into the valley. In the distance, they saw the smoke from a chimney in town, saw it spiral upwards, hit a draft of air and fan out, hang motionless over Pipestone, a marker for any to see who ventured over the pass.

Once they heard a volley of shots down below and then it was still. Slocum headed the horses downslope.

"Where are we going now?" asked Norman.

"We're going hunting," said Slocum.

Skaggs barked his orders quickly, sending men back to town, others up to close off the pass. Still others he sent out in roving patrols, three men apiece, and gave them a pattern to follow. He was very good at this kind of warfare, and the men all knew it. Some had been with him along the Arkansas-Missouri border and they knew better than anyone how good he was.

"Rufus," he said, "I want you to take a detail of men and bring all them bodies back up here to the pass."

"Up here?"

"Yeah. I want them Vigilantes to know what's what."

"Be like boards, Emmett."

"Want 'em to see 'em real clear."

"Anything else?"

"Watch real keerful."

Harding nodded, looked up at the towering parapets that rose over the narrow pass. He waved to men he saw there, standing guard. He caught up his horse, called to Nate Bonstall, who stood behind a cluster of rocks near the entrance to the pass. Nate stood up, walked over to him.

"Need two more men, at least, to go back to town."

"Better'n sittin' here in the sun," said Bonstall.

"You won't think so when you see what we got to do."

Emmett Skaggs watched the men ride off down to the valley, thought about the time he got caught in the battle of Pea Ridge down in Arkansas during the war. He and his bunch had pretty well been living off the land, but he never thought the Union troops would come down that far to stop the rebel advance way back in sixty-two. It was a hell of a time, a hell of a battle around Elk Horn Tavern. Artillery, cavalry, infantry, both sides had used them all.

The War had taught Emmett a lot, but mostly it had taught him logistics. An army couldn't fight without food and ammunition. No man could, either. Keep your supply lines open. Skaggs had food and ammunition caches all along his route in and out of the valley, and at strategic locations on the old Bozeman Trail, as well. Always keep an ace in the hole.

There were other things he had learned during the War, too. Like the advantage of surprise. The guerrilla warrior used shock and maneuverability to make up for an inferior force. Stay mobile. Keep moving. Do things the more highly disciplined enemy would not do. Stay off the main roads, keep to the woods. Blend into the countryside when pursued.

Keep the flanks flexible. In and out, swell and shrink. confuse the enemy whenever possible.

That was how Skaggs learned to fight and survive during the War and that was what gave him confidence now. The Vigilantes who had attacked his town were poorly prepared, he knew. They had come in shooting, hoping to throw, tie, and brand in ten minutes. They had no supplies, no reserves. Now they had taken to the timber, but they would have to come out sometime. They would have to come to the only road in or out and they would have to try for the pass.

He smiled to himself as he thought about these things.

Meanwhile, he had his scouts out and the Vigilantes were, he knew, scattered. Each time a Vigilante encountered trouble it would be at least three against one. Keep your units small and mobile. That was what he had learned. Those were the tactics he was using now, and it gave him great satisfaction.

All through the afternoon, his men rode in and out of his stronghold at the pass, giving reports. He heard scattered rifle and pistol fire and as the men rode in, he knew that the vigilantes were being picked off one by one.

"Bring the bodies up here," he ordered. "Lay them across the trail. Let them stink. Let the buzzards gather until the sky is dark with 'em."

That was what they did. Bonstall brought up the horses with the dead ranchers laid across them. Six, seven, eight, nine, the pile of bodies grew.

Skaggs's men hunted down the ranchers. They shot them on the roads, in the timber. They chased them along the creeks and up on the ridges.

Slocum heard it happening, saw Skaggs's men bring the bodies in, one by one, stretch the dead out on the road over the pass. Norman drew back in horror when Slocum showed him the grisly sight.

"He's killing them all," he said. "Every last one of them."

"Skaggs is pretty good at this kind of fighting," Slocum admitted. "It's only a matter of time until he gets us, too."

"What can we do? He's got that pass blocked. We couldn't slip through there, even at night."

"No," said Slocum. He lay on the flat of the ridge, looking down at Skaggs's stronghold, saw the men come and go, always in threes. "Pretty soon they'll make a sweep and catch us up in their net. We've got to get you out of here."

"What about you?"

"I think one man might have a chance to wear them down. They can count, and I'm pretty sure Skaggs knows how many of you rode in here. If he kills all of your men, he'll know there's only two of us left. If I can get you out, you can bring reinforcements."

"I thought that pass was the only way in or out of here," said Norman.

"No. There's another way, a harder way."

"What's that?"

"The way I came in," said Slocum, and he scooted back off the ridge. Norman followed him to their horses.

Skaggs was counting. As the dead began to pile up, he gloated. He began to lose his smile, though, when Slocum wasn't among any of those dead men being brought in.

"Where in hell is that bastard?" he asked.

No one could tell him. But he began to worry. He increased the size of his patrols to five men.

"Fan out, stay forty yards apart. Sweep the ridges, comb the gullies. That bastard is out there somewhere. And he's with Lou Norman or I'm not Emmett William Skaggs."

Skaggs had had a brush with Norman and his quarter-circle N ranchers before. But he never thought he'd bring in Vigilantes to help him fight back. It didn't make any difference, though. Norman may have kept most of his beef, but he was on the losing side, nevertheless.

"We've run acrost some tracks," said Wales. "Could be them. Looks like they been close. Close enough to see the pass."

"One man or two?"

"Two together," said Wales. Jethro affirmed the assessment with a nod of his own.

"Good," said Skaggs. "I want them to get a good look. Any idea where they're headed?"

"They always seem a jump ahead of us," said Wales. "They been holding to the trees, stayin' just below the ridges. Walkin' their horses slow so they don't make much of a track."

"Slocum's tricky," said Bonstall. "He might try to pull something."

"He might do something fancy," agreed Harding.

"Well, you just be ready," said Skaggs, frowning. Slocum was the unknown factor. If he was leading the parade, calling the shots, they could be in for some surprises. "I want the town locked up tight. Post guards at Pete Anders's place, 'round the clock. Shoot Norman and Slocum on sight, hear?"

The men around him nodded.

Skaggs looked up at the skyline, down at the valley. Slocum was in there somewhere. And he was scheming. Trying to find a way out. Skaggs couldn't let that happen. No one on the outside must ever find out about Pipestone. He had to find Slocum, and kill him.

He looked at the other men around him, concealed behind rocks, hiding in bushes. If Slocum came to them, he'd never get through. But Skaggs would give anything to know what Slocum was thinking at that very moment.

Slocum saw the five riders, pulled his horse behind a blue spruce, motioned for Norman to hold steady. Two of the men were looking at the ground, reading sign. The other three were scanning both sides of the game trail. They had their rifles at the ready. Slocum froze, watched the trackers. He recognized them. Haskins and Tinker.

He and Norman had crossed that game path an hour ago and now must cross it again. Beyond lay the Crow trail, the one he had come in on, afoot. That was the way he had come in, and that was the way he figured to get Norman back out. But the riders were thick now, crossing and re-crossing their trails, picking up sign. It was only a matter of time before Bonstall, Harding, or one of the others fig-ured things out.

Slocum debated with himself whether or not to shoot it out with the five men. If they managed to ride through, they'd have Skaggs's men down on them like hornets. No, it was best to lay low, stay quiet, and wait for them to pass, then slip on past them. He tried to remember where they had crossed the game trail. Closer to town? Closer to the pass?

The riders decided for him. They picked up the tracks closer to town, and now they veered off the trail and headed upslope, toward the ridge. Slocum held his breath. They hadn't made such a wide loop. Depending upon how good the trackers were, they didn't have much time.

Slocum waited until he could no longer hear the outlaw horses going through the timber. He signalled to Norman to follow him. He picked his way carefully down to the game trail, crossed it, then angled southwest on a course that would take him below the town.

Norman followed Slocum, blindingly, trustingly. Slo-cum angled off their path more southerly. They heard three shots off in the direction of the pass, and then it was quiet once again. Norman winced at each shot, as if knowing that another of his men would join those lying dead up at the pass. Slocum continued his relentless ride through dense brush and thick tree stands, following some blind path away from the town.

Soon they came to a path that Norman recognized as one used by both men and game. But the hoofprints were from unshod horses. A feeling of dread began to come over him as they rode through dense timber, farther and farther into the valley toward low hills barely visible in the distance.

Soon they came to a wide spot, a clearing by a stream, but before they got there, Norman could smell the place. Buzzards flapped up as they approached the dead bodies of the Crow Indians. Norman held his nose.

"What is this?" he asked nasally.

"Crow. This is the way I came in. This is the way you'll get out."

"Who killed them?"

"I did," said Slocum, without explanation.

They rode past the carcasses, which had been picked over by buzzards, coyotes, rats, and insects. Norman looked at a grinning skull and fought to keep from throwing up. Soon, they passed the place of the dead Crow and the trail widened, wound through open spots, crossed small streams. There were many tracks of game and high grass in the meadows. Norman kept looking back over his shoulder, over to the pass with its high parapets. He saw the buzzards floating over the rimrock and he shuddered.

"You follow this trail, Norman," said Slocum, reining up at the far edge of an open meadow. "It will lead you back up to the Bozeman. From there, you can find your way to Virginia City. You already know your way in through the pass."

"You want us to come in that way?"

"It might be easier, quicker."

"What are you going to do?"

"I'm going to double back."

"That's almost certain death," said Norman, now convinced that Slocum was not only honest, but an extraordinary man.

"Maybe. I have an idea to go back in there the same way I came in, with a little ace in the hole."

"They'll shoot you on sight."

"Oh, I'm going to hunt my way in," Slocum said mysteriously. "When you return with help, you take up a point where you can see the sky over Pipestone. Don't ride in like you did before, shooting and yelling. When you see some black smoke hanging over the town, you come running. That'll mean I need help, but the odds will be a little more in your favor."

"I don't understand," said Norman.

"Trust me." Slocum grinned. "I'll give you a week. Can you make it back by then?"

"Sooner, maybe. I've ridden hard before and I've left a remuda up on the trail, some men to watch after them."

"Better get going then," said Slocum. "I'll see you inside of a week."

"You can count on it," said Norman, squaring his jaw.

Slocum watched him ride off through the trees. Buffalo had made this trail a long time ago and the Indians had used it. It was broad enough for Norman to follow without any trouble.

Soon, it was quiet, and Slocum rode back to the place of the dead Crow. He knew what he was facing. He would have to live off the land for five days, a week. And, he would have to cut down the odds before Normans's return.

To do that, he would not only have to stay alive, he would have to kill.

Grimly, he rode on.

12

Slocum stayed near the dead Crow for two days. The smell bothered him some, but after a while either he got used to it or it went away. He slept in brush that clogged a small ravine, kept the horse on grass some distance away, hobbled so he could catch him up when he needed to. He wanted Skaggs to start sweating.

Once he saw Bonstall and Harding following his and Norman's tracks, but he knew they'd never find his coming back. He made sure of that, staying to hard ground and brushing away those on soft. It rained the second night and that was the end of the tracking. By then, he knew that Skaggs would think he and Norman had gotten clean away and would be riding hard for help. Unless he missed his guess, Skaggs would be fortifying the town, getting ready for any Vigilante raids that might come his way.

On the third day, Slocum walked back toward town. He was careful about his tracks and took his time. As he had told Norman, he was going back to Pipestone the way he had come in, on foot. He didn't want to present a big target and he didn't want men on horseback chasing him. He wanted to pick his men carefully, catch them off guard, alone.

Slocum watched the town from the fringe of trees for a long time that afternoon. He saw men coming and going, riding around the town carrying rifles and shotguns, in pairs and threes. A gunman he didn't know, but had seen in town, came out back of the stables to wash in the trough after such a ride and Slocum slipped up on him. He ringnecked him, then put his head in the trough, held it down. The man kicked for several seconds, then sucked in air and it was all over. Slocum left him there in the trough, half in and half out, slumped over. That was where Nate Wales found him an hour later.

"Charlie's dead!" he yelled, and men came running. Slocum watched them, heard them mutter and argue. But no one could really say how Charlie had died and Slocum never did hear his last name.

Late that afternoon, one of the outriders dropped back and dismounted to check one of the shoes on his mount. The other two riders rode ahead and didn't look back. Slocum came up to the man, called his name.

"Howdy, Jethro. Remember me?"

Jethro turned around and Slocum shot him just as he slapped leather. The ball struck Dekins square between the eyes, blew his brains out the back of his head. Before Dekins hit the ground, Slocum was running into the trees. He had disappeared by the time the other two riders came back to see what had happened. Dekins lay sprawled on the ground, facedown, a hole in his forehead, the back of his head blown away like a pie plate.

"Holy shit," said one man.

"Somebody dusted off Deke."

"And got clean away."

They turned Jethro Dekins over, saw the powder burns on his face.

"No more'n two foot away, I'd say."

"Christ."

Slocum circled the town, watched the riders comb the woods on the other side for him. He listened to the crackling of brush, heard the whicker of horses as men crossed and recrossed each other's trails. He waited for nightfall, lying low in thick brush, both pistols fully loaded, extra cylinders loaded and capped, as well.

Emmett Skaggs looked at the group of men assembled in the saloon. On his orders, the bar was closed. The men sat at tables, or on the floor, leaned against the bar and the walls, and listened as Skaggs larruped into them with an angry tirade.

"They're making fools of you. Two men. Two goddamned men and they're runnin' you in circles, killin'. Two damned men and you can't bring me their miserable hides. Slocum and Norman have got you all spooked. I don't like it, men. I don't like it a damned bit."

"Emmett," said Bonstall, "beggin' your pardon, but it ain't two men."

"Huh? You're saying there's more of 'em?" Emmett's face was florid from anger and he stopped pacing to regard this latest bearer of heresy.

"No," said Bonstall self-consciously, fidgeting with the kerchief around his neck. He looked at Haskins, who looked quickly away. There would be no support there.

"What in hell is it, then?"

"I'm sayin' that it ain't Norman. He got clean away, I'm pretty sure."

"So, who's killin' our friends, Nate?"

"Slocum," said Bonstall. "Just Slocum."

Skaggs started to laugh, then caught himself up short. He stared at Bonstall for a long time. Then he looked at Haskins. Haskins nodded slowly. He was the best tracker Skaggs had.

"You sayin' that Slocum is doin' this all by hisself?"

"Yeah," said Bonstall.

It grew very quiet in the saloon, then. Skaggs looked at his men and saw that they were struck with wonder and with shame. The sun was going down and only a few men were still out hunting what appeared to be a lone man.

"Well, what are we going to do about Slocum?" asked Skaggs. He spoke more to himself than the men in the saloon. "He's just pickin' us off, one by one."

Skaggs looked hard at Haskins, then at Tinker.

"The man don't track easy," said Tinker. Haskins nodded.

"Hell," said Jethro Caudill, with bravado, "he's just like any other man. I'll bet I could bring him down."

Skaggs's eyes rolled in their sockets.

"He done pinned your ears back, once, boy," said Bonstall. "Best you stay out'n his way."

"Me and Bonstall could kill Slocum easy if we had the chance," said Harding.

"All of you are just whistlin' in the dark," said Skaggs. "I want patrols on the street tonight. On foot. Stay in the shadows; don't take any chances. Tomorrow, I want riders out beatin' the brush. I want armed guards lockin' up the town tight. No one goes in or out, hear?"

The men in the saloon muttered and murmured, but they nodded obediently.

"I'm tired of Slocum makin' us look like fools," said Skaggs. "The man that kills him gets five hunnert dollars cash."

The men in the saloon let out a whoop and Skaggs opened the bar.

Pete Anders heard the cheering from the bar as he locked up shop. He and Alice exchanged wary glances. They had been on edge all day. Sally came out from the back where she had been dusting, washing windows. Jack Lovelace stood on guard out front, a dry man licking his lips as he looked longingly at the saloon.

"I've never seen Skaggs running scared before," said Pete.

"I don't think he's scared, just mad," said Alice.

"I'm scared," said Sally. "Pa, what's going to happen now? John Slocum can't stand up to all these men by himself."

"He's been doing all right so far," said her father. "But I'm worried, too. Come, let's go home and fix supper. Maybe Slocum will try to come in tonight."

"If he does, we could all be killed," said Alice, and the way she said it, flat and toneless, made her brother worry that she was more unsettled than she seemed. The terrible shootout that morning, the sight of the dead being carried up to the pass on skittery horses had made them all nervous. But Alice seemed to be fighting off a deep depression. Pete put his arm around her shoulders and drew her to him.

Don't worry about Slocum," he said. "He won't put us in danger."

Slocum heard the cheering from the saloon, too, and he wondered about it. He wondered if Melanie Lovelace was inside, listening to the talk. He had seen the men go there, had seen Jack, her father, guarding the Anders store, knew something must be up.

He waited another hour, saw the shadows of men walking the streets, checking as they went along.

Let them sweat, he thought, and left his lookout position on a craggy outcropping above the town and walked to where he had the black gelding hobbled. He needed a good night's rest. He was hungry, but he would not eat this night. He had thinking to do, and he must find a place to sleep that was secure.

Melanie Lovelace slipped across the darkened street carrying a bundle in her hand. Furtively, she approached the man standing in the shadows.

"You bring it?" rasped Jack Lovelace.

"Yes, but Pa, if Emmett finds out . . ."

"He won't, less'n you tell him. Give me the bottle."

Melanie handed her father the cloth sack holding the bottle of whiskey. She watched as her father pulled the cork and tipped the bottle up to his mouth. She heard the liquid gurgle down his throat. He coughed, caught his breath, and drank again. He wiped his lips with his sleeve, swayed slightly in the darkness.

"Aren't you supposed to be over to the Anders place?" she asked.

"I'll be there directly. They just went to home a few minutes ago."

"Pa, I—I'm scared."

"Of who? Slocum?"

"I'm afraid of what they'll do to him."

"I'll do to him if I see him."

"Pa . . . Slocum's a good man."

"We'll see how good he is," Lovelace said sarcastically. "You'd best get him out of your mind."

"I—I think I love him, Pa."

Jack lashed out then, slapped his daughter hard across

the mouth. She cried out, staggered backwards, holding her jaw in her hand.

"Don't talk like a slut," Jack warned. "I'm goin' to kill that bastard."

"Oh, Pa, can't you see what you're doing is wrong? Can't you see that decent folks don't want this kind of life? Are you blind?"

"Get out of here," he slurred. "Get back to work."

Melanie stifled a sob. She looked at the pale light on her father's face, saw the mask he wore, the pain underneath. She didn't know what drove him to do the things he did, but she knew he must be in an awful torment because of the way he lashed out at her. She knew he had to be hurting terribly bad inside to hate the way he did. He hated himself worst of all, she knew, but he wouldn't change. Now, more than ever, she knew he wouldn't change, and his hate would carry him right to his grave.

She ran off, then, back across the street, slipped between two buildings to come up behind the Pipestone Saloon. She was sobbing by the time she reached the back door. She paused there, looked up at the backbone of the mountains looming in the darkness, reaching to the velvet sky. Usually they gave her comfort, but not tonight. Slocum was out there somewhere and, tomorrow, Emmett's men would hunt him down. And her father would be one of them. She hoped Slocum wouldn't be killed, but in her heart she knew she had an even deeper, more somber dread.

She hoped that Slocum wouldn't kill Jack Lovelace, her father. Hateful as he was, she loved him. And, now, she was sure she loved John Slocum, as well.

Sobbing, she went inside, wiping her eyes, straightening her dress.

She put on a bright smile and danced into the arena to

serve her customers. The tears in her eyes made them shine bright as stars, and that night she looked more beautiful than she ever had before.

Rufus Harding ran the cleaning rod down the barrel of his mountain rifle, checked the patch. Satisfied, he popped a cap to dry it out, snapped another to make sure. Then he measured out ninety grains of black powder, poured it down the barrel. He slapped the stock at the receiver to make sure the powder settled. He patched a ball measuring .490 and started it down the barrel with a short starter. Then he rammed it home with his ramrod, made sure the ball and patch were seated. He capped the nipple, put the hammer on half-cock, and leaned it against the door of his room.

Nate Bonstall looked up from cleaning his pistol. The room smelled of oil and lead and black powder.

"Finished?" he asked.

"I cleaned both my pistols. Wished I had me a Henry, like you."

"They're mighty heavy to lug around all day."

"I might need more than one shot, Nate."

"Not if it's the right shot."

Harding laughed. Bonstall always knew the right thing to say. This Slocum business was getting him down, more than it was Nate. He had liked the man, had hoped they would ride together, become friends. Now, he was the enemy. He couldn't figure it. Man like Slocum was always on the prod, just one step away from the law.

"Why you reckon Slocum turned on us like he did?" he asked Bonstall.

"I don't know," said Nate. "Man like that's hard to figure. He strikes me as a loner. Maybe he wants it all for hisself."

"Could be. I was hopin' he'd ride with us."

"Well, Rufe, we got to kill him now."

Harding let the silence fill up the room. There was only the sound of Nate's oilcloth sliding up and down the barrel of his Remington sixgun.

"I know," said Rufus. "Like a goddamned mad dog."

"Yeah," said Bonstall. He stopped wiping the pistol, set it down on the table where he sat. He looked at Harding a long time.

"What you thinking, Nate?"

"You know what I'm thinking, Rufus? I'm thinking you and me could split that five hunnert dollars. You could buy yourself a brand-new Henry, get some fancy duds, take a trip back East."

"Yeah, I could, couldn't I? What you got in mind, Nate?"

"You and me can take Slocum down. I been thinkin' a lot about how he gave us all the slip today. You know what I think he done?"

"Naw."

"Look, he come in here over that Injun trail. Nobody much goes that way 'cause it goes right through Crow country. I bet he doubled back, went thataway, knowing nobody'd foller him."

Harding's countenance lit up.

"You know, I think you might be right, Nate! Hell, I never thought about it. He don't know no part of the country but that, and that's mighty likely the place he'd go to get out of trouble."

"I keep wondering why him and that Norman feller didn't just ride on out and keep a-goin'."

"I was thinkin' the same thing," Harding said, although he had never thought of it until just then. Bonstall was the thinker. He always knew what to say and when to say it, too. That was why Harding liked him so much. He could think and he knew what to say.

"Maybe this Slocum ran into Emmett before, you reckon? Maybe it warn't no accident he come in here like he did."

"I don't see where you're going, Nate."

"Well, if Slocum's staying around, trying to kill us all, maybe Emmett done him some wrong one time. Like that Norman feller. We took out a herd of his quartercircle N beeves once't before, you recollec'."

"Yair, I do. Fine beeves."

"So, maybe Slocum was in a party we hit sometime back."

"You reckon?"

"I reckon that's it."

"Then it must be so, Nate. Hell, it's the onliest thing that makes any sense at all."

"Yeah, I reckon. So, what say we go out early tomorry on our own and see if we can't run Slocum to ground. Go back to where them poisoned Crows lay and see if we can't scratch his trail."

"Damn, Nate, I'd like that all right. Hell, we can take Slocum. Sneak right up on him."

"Got to be careful, though. The man's trickier'n a shed-skin rattler."

"We'll go real quiet."

"Better get some shut-eye, Rufe. I want to get started awful early."

"I don't know if I can sleep. That five hunnert dollars would be mighty fine to have."

"Well, you keep a-thinkin' that, Rufe. Tomorry, we'll bring in Slocum's hide, tack it to the wall."

Harding walked over to his bunk, sat down, and started pulling at his boots. He wore a big grin on his face. Bonstall began loading the cylinders of his Remington New Model Army converted to cartridge. He wouldn't mind having one of those new Henrys himself.

Emmett Skaggs remembered the soldiers riding along the Wire Road. Union troops. He rode off to report what he'd seen and the next day, he saw some of the battle when the Confederates came in behind the Union lines up on Pea Ridge, swarming down on Elk Horn Tavern. They might have won that day, too, if they hadn't run out of ammunition. Van Dorn should have let the ammunition wagons come on through, but he turned them back.

Emmett had ridden off, then, taken booty from dead Union soldiers, joining back up with his band of free soilers who didn't join either side. But, he had worked as a scout for the Confederates a little, and he used that to advantage now and again. Later, when the Union won, he told folks he had fought on that side, but he never had. He had seen men like Slocum, though, riding with Quantrill. Maybe Slocum himself, even, but he couldn't recollect for sure. That was a long time ago and he had forgotten a lot of the things that had happened back then. He remembered seeing the woods all torn up from artillery fire, and the burned towns, the smudged faces of the people standing on scorched land, in rubble, their fields torn up, their stock run off, stolen, or killed in battle.

He didn't want anything like that to happen to Pipestone. He turned down the lamp and sat for a long time looking out the window, smelling the scent of cedar and pines and juniper, the thick aroma of spruce and fir coming down from the mountain. No, he had to stop Slocum, kill him, and if Norman ever showed up again, he'd have to kill him, too, and those who rode with him.

Pipestone was his home, now. His fortress. No man was

going to spoil it for him. Not Norman, not Slocum.

For Emmett Skaggs, it was war all over again. But this time, he was fighting for his home.

He cursed softly in the darkness, rolled over on his bed, and closed his eyes.

But he did not sleep.

He kept seeing Slocum's face and trying to remember if he had ever seen the man before.

13

Slocum set the snares just before dawn, when it was light enough to see, along the game paths. He had done much the same as a boy in Georgia. He used leather thongs he had gathered the night before from the Crow camp, cut from the leather breechclouts that lay in tatters near the skeletons. He had salvaged what he could, from their clothes and the things they carried with them.

When the snares were set, Slocum caught up the black and rode away from that part of the timber. He washed himself, drank in the stream. He was hungry and began gathering firewood, the driest and leanest he could find, stacking it under a big spruce. With his knife, he cut away the lower limbs. He gathered squaw wood to start the fire. From the Crow, he had flint and steel, tinder. When he built his fire, the smoke would go up through the spruce bows and dissipate. He didn't think anyone in Pipestone would see the smoke. He was far enough away that he knew they would not smell it. By the time he was finished, his stomach was gnawing at him. He had jumped a rabbit at the stream, but even if he had fired, it was too quick. He would have missed and someone would probably have heard the shot. Right now, he needed this place as a hideout and shelter. Later on, maybe, someone would think to come this way looking for him, but for now, he had it all to himself.

He sucked in the clean air of morning, watched the sun rise slowly, spread colors over the gentle rolling hills, turn the dark knolls to tawny gold as the eastern sky lightened and the stars faded away.

Slocum looked around him, listened to the sounds of morning, saw the buzzards rising up from their roosts to catch the early zephyrs. He saw two of them float over the Crow camp, drop below the trees, then rise upward again, flapping hard to overcome inertia. Something was wrong, he reasoned. Something had startled the birds. Something was there that should not be there, had not been there when he passed through the night before.

Suddenly there was something ominous about the morning, even though the sky was blue and the air clear, full of the scent of balsam and pine. Slocum rode toward the Crow camp, making a wide circle, keeping to the trees, stopping often to listen for an alien sound. He wondered about his own camp, wondered if he had forgotten anything important, left any sign of where he had spent the last few nights.

Some parts of his body were still sore from sleeping on the ground. One of his shoulders ached slightly, and a rib or two hurt when he moved a certain way. But he had slept well, and was rested. As he rode, he worked the kinks out, flexed the muscles of his arm and shoulder until they worked smoothly. He didn't want to make any serious mistakes if somebody was onto his trail.

Rufus Harding watched the buzzards descend onto the Crow braves' last camp on earth. The place smelled, but not so bad as he had expected. When he and Bonstall rode into the clearing, the buzzards flapped upwards, pumping for altitude, and he laughed low in his throat.

"Just like we left it," he said.

"No," said Bonstall. "Somebody's been here." He looked at the grisly skeletons, saw that loincloths had been stripped away. There were tracks, too, fresh. Boot heels sunk into earth where a man had stepped carefully, but not carefully enough. The place held the awesome quiet of death, like a lonely graveyard, with the morning breeze rustling through the grasses, whining low through the rib bones that had almost been picked clean by scavenging wildlife.

"Yeah. Slocum, likely."

"He took what he needed, looks like." Bonstall leaned over the side of his dun horse, surveyed the decayed remains of the Crow, the maze of tracks. He sat up straight, after a few moments, looked at Harding.

"We'd best split up, make a circle, see where those boot tracks go. Slocum's been here, all right. I'd swear to it."

"Yeah," said Harding, once again impressed by his partner's keen powers of observation. He had not seen much, fascinated by the grinning skulls with shreds of flesh still clinging to the bones, the empty ribcages.

He took the south side, Bonstall, the north. They rode around the circumference of the clearing. Harding disappeared into the timber, looking for broken twigs, boot tracks. Bonstall switched back and forth, finally found a track to the east, followed it, leaning over to one side so that he could look close at the ground from no more than three feet away. A muscle in his jaw began to twitch when he picked up the hazy trail of a man walking toward the rising sun.

He thought of calling Harding over, but the tracks were so fresh, they excited him. Last night's, from the looks of them, and he saw that the man who had made them had been careful, stepping lightly, going into thick brush, sometimes ducking under the low branches of spruce, sometimes doubling back, taking hard oblique angles, but always pushing eastward. Bonstall's heart began to pound with a definite, audible beat in his chest. He was tracking a good man, he knew, and a man who was armed. He began to look ahead now, and slowed his horse's pace. He began to feel like someone was breathing down the back of his neck. He touched his hand to the butt of his pistol, uneasy, wary. Sweat began to sleek his forehead, slick his back. Deer flies swarmed over him, their gray bodies nearly invisible against the dust imbedded in his dark trousers. He felt their tiny stings and swatted at them quietly, afraid to make noise. The dun switched his tail, sending the flies carouseling up into the air, swick, swick, and the sound was like the ticking of an erratic clock. It made Bonstall nervous, as if he was waiting for a dynamite bomb to go off at any moment.

Harding roamed in the blind, circling, cutting Bonstall's trail, but never seeing him. He rode wider on a spiralling path, but he saw no sign that he could recognize. He felt lost. He never was much good at tracking. He could follow blood and deep hoofmarks, but that was about all. He was never good at finding deer rubs or scrapes. He never knew where to look. Now, he fought at the deer flies that clouded around him like moving smoke, swatted at them when they bit into his legs, drove needles into his back. He cursed under his breath, slapped at his neck, felt the soft bodies crush bloody under his fingers. It was getting hot already and sweat dripped down from his brows, burned his eyes. He wiped his forehead with his bandanna, tucked it back in his pocket, half-blinded, still, the woods a blur of green, and rising morning mist.

Slocum slipped out of the saddle, quiet. He hobbled the black horse in gamma grass, stalked through the woods towards the sounds he'd heard. He stepped carefully, avoided the slap of brush, the crunch of rock underfoot. Somewhere ahead he heard a horse moving through the timber, heard its hooves crack dry, dead branches. It sounded, he thought, like a bull elk feeding.

He saw Rufus Harding through the trees. It was then that he heard another horse off to his right, heard it whicker and the sound cut off as if someone had cuffed it across its soft nose. Slocum froze, watched Harding continue his circular path toward him. When Harding broke into the open, some forty yards away, Slocum stepped from behind the tree, one of the Navy Colts fisted in his hand.

"Looking for something?" he asked softly.

Harding jerked up straight in the saddle, grabbed for his rifle.

"Slocum!"

Before Slocum could say anything, Harding brought his rifle up to his shoulder, cocked the hammer back. Slocum raised his arm, cocking the pistol. He heard the click of the set trigger on Harding's rifle and then it was too late to stop his own actions. He squeezed the trigger of the Colt as the front blade sight lined up with the rear notch in the center of Harding's breastbone. The light pull gave as Slocum ticked his finger and the pistol bucked in his hand. Flaming orange sparks spit from the muzzle and a cloud of white smoke obscured his target, but he heard Harding grunt. A split-second later, the mountain rifle boomed and a lead ball cut the air with a whooshing sound like a knife cutting through leaves.

Slocum stepped quickly to one side, away from the smoke, saw Harding drop the smoking rifle, twist grotesquely in the saddle. His arms flailed for a moment as if he were dropping off a high cliff and then he pitched over headfirst, tumbled from the saddle. He hit the ground hard, rolled over, and lay flat on his back. Slocum ran up to him, cocking on the run, and looked down at the mortally wounded man. The ball had severed the artery leading into the aorta. Blood pumped through the small, dark hole. Harding's eyes glazed over with a dull film, glistened in the glint of sunlight. His mouth moved, but no sound came out. Slocum eased the hammer back down as Harding twitched one last time and his eyes remained fixed in a deathlock. A last shudder and the blood stopped pumping through the shattered artery. Harding's horse bent its neck, set to grazing a few yards away.

Bonstall heard the shots. They were so close together he was not sure which he had heard first; the light, sharp crack of the pistol exploding ten or twelve grains of black powder, or the boom of the mountain rifle loaded up with ninety grains of medium fine. But he knew Harding had run into something and he marked the sounds, clapped spurs to the dun's flanks. He drew his pistol, ducked his head as the horse raced through the timber.

He smelled smoke, brought the dun up to a walk with a quick haul-in on the reins. It was quiet now and Bonstall wondered why. If Harding had gotten Slocum he would have cried out, shouted. Yet no one called. What had happened? There were two shots, he was sure of that. Close together. One pistol, the other, Rufus' .50 caliber.

Somewhere, in the distance, Nate heard the high-pitched *scree* of the hunting hawk, and close at hand, only the swick-swick of the dun's tail. He looked through the timber in every direction, still heading for the place where he had heard the two shots. Some warning rustle in his brain told him to get the hell out of there, but something else, a burning curiosity, perhaps, or a fascination with danger, urged him on. Moments later, he saw Harding's horse grazing, its reins trailing on the ground.

A second or two after that, he heard his name called.

"Bonstall, hold up," said the voice, and Nate stiffened, recognizing it at once.

He looked for the speaker, swinging his pistol in the direction of the voice.

"Drop it," said Slocum.

"Fuck your mother," said Bonstall tightly. He hammered back, pointed the Remington pistol toward a tree.

Slocum wasn't right where Bonstall expected him to be. Instead, he came out low, squatting, and his pistol cracked, spat smoke and flame. Bonstall felt a hard smack on his arm, as if someone had swung a sixteen-pound maul square at the bone. He heard the bone crack and his pistol fell from suddenly distended fingers.

He cried out in pain and grabbed his elbow, felt the jagged splinters of bone. Blood slicked his fingers. The pain subsided for a moment as the shock triggered chemicals into his blood. His stomach turned with a sudden sickness and the trees spun overhead as a dizziness assailed him.

Slocum stood up, approached with the smoking Colt in his hand.

"Light down, Bonstall," he said, "before you fall out of the saddle."

"Wh—where's Rufus?" Bonstall asked idiotically.

"Lying dead over there."

"You son of a bitch, why don't you go ahead and finish me?"

"I want you to deliver a message," said Slocum, looking up at the man in the saddle. Bonstall's face was chalk-white, drained of color. He swayed in the saddle, his eyes blinking as he tried to focus.

Slocum pulled on the wounded man's good arm, and Bonstall tumbled from the saddle like a sack of meal. Slocum caught him before he hit the ground, braced himself for the dead weight of the man. Bonstall reeled, off-balance, but managed to keep his feet when Slocum released him.

Now the pain rushed into Bonstall's arm, bringing tears to his eyes. He stood there, grimacing, trying to hold up his shattered arm, swaying back and forth, his eyes closing and opening like errant shutters in a high wind.

"Christ," he said. "Christ."

"You'll heal," said Slocum. He saw that the wound was bad, but neither artery in the arm had been severed. There was splintered bone jutting out of the broken elbow, plenty of blood, but it wasn't spurting, just bubbling out slowly.

"What in hell do you want, Slocum?"

"I want Skaggs. I want you to give him a message from me."

"Hell, he'll have men in here on top of you before you can get five miles away," said Bonstall defiantly.

"I'm not going anywhere," said Slocum.

"Better yet. He's got men to spare who will hunt you down."

"I'll be coming to Pipestone," Slocum told him.

"Yeah?"

"Yeah. You tell Skaggs I'm coming and that from now

on, Pipestone is under law. My law. You got that?"

"I don't know what you're talking about. You the law?"

"For now, I am. I'm the law."

Bonstall looked at Slocum crookedly for a long moment. He shook his head and shuttered with the sudden resurgence of pain in his arm.

"You've got sand, Slocum, or else you're plumb loco. There ain't no law in Pipestone. The joke's on you."

"There is now," said Slocum. "Now mount up and ride out of here before I change my mind and shoot you where you stand."

"What about Harding?"

"You can take him back. Mount up."

Slocum stripped the saddlebags from the dun, took Bonstall's Henry repeating rifle from its sheath. He helped the wounded man into the saddle, tucked the fallen Remington into his belt.

He caught up Harding's horse, led him to the dead man. He hefted Harding's corpse onto the saddle, tied him tight with Rufus's own rope. He gave the reins to Bonstall, slapped the dun on the rump. Bonstall rode off toward Pipestone. Slocum sighed, carried the saddlebags with him, picked up Harding's rifle and broke it over a deadfall, left it where it fell.

He watched Bonstall disappear in the timber, waited another ten minutes before going after the black. A half hour later, he checked his snares. They were empty, and his stomach growled in protest. He searched through Bonstall's saddlebags, found ammunition for the Henry, a piece of dried beefsteak and hardtack, wrapped in a swatch of oilcloth. He gnawed the dry food into saliva-soaked paste, swallowed it with effort. He swallowed a lot of water, but his hunger did not go away.

* * *

By the time Bonstall reached Pipestone, he was giddy from
the loss of blood. The town glistened under a pall of morning smoke from the cook fires. The smell of new wood
smelled rotten, somehow, as if it were wormy, or sodden
from rain. He rode in, heard the shouted questions from
blurred men who sounded as though they were talking with
wads of cotton stuffed in their mouths. Someone grabbed
the reins of Harding's horse from his hands, and a pair of
men helped him out of the saddle.

"Got to see Emmett," he said, then fainted dead away.
He felt himself falling, but he never hit the ground.

They poured raw whiskey down his throat, set his arm,
and stuffed the wound with salve, wrapped it tight. Bonstall gritted his teeth against the pain, drank the whiskey
like water as men stood around him, glint-eyed and wondering. Skaggs came into the saloon, then, looked at Bonstall sitting on one of the tables, reeking of alcohol and
medicants."

"What the hell's goin' on?" he roared.

The men made a path for Skaggs and he stepped up to
Bonstall, looked at him without pity.

"Slocum killed Rufus," said Bonstall. "Shot me in the
arm."

"Why in hell didn't he kill you, too?" Skaggs asked, the
belligerence plain in his voice.

"He wanted me to deliver you a message."

"What?"

"He said to tell you he was the law come to Pipestone."

"The law? What goddamned law?"

"That's what he said, Emmett. He said he'd be coming
here to get you."

Emmett's face turned nearly purple with rage. His eyes

bulged from their sockets and his neck swelled like a rutting bull's.

"Well, let the son of a bitch come," said Skaggs. "We'll be waiting for the bastard. Haskins, you get Caudill and some other boys set up on the roofs where you can see a long ways. Tinker, you seal off this town tight. Pull in all roving patrols."

"Boss," said Tinker, "we're runnin' mighty low on supplies, food and such. I checked with Anders this mornin' and we can't last more'n a day or so less'n we get some meat and staples in."

"I don't want to hear about it," said Skaggs. "Anyways, it won't be more'n a couple of days before we get Slocum. Tell you what, boys, I'll up the price on his head to one thousand. Make that two thousand if you get him before sundown. And I do mean his head. I want it cut off and brought to me. I'll show that son of a bitch."

Skaggs looked at Bonstall with disgust. He and Harding had had their chance, and they caved in like yellowbellies when Slocum came after them. Bonstall shrank away from the withering look and Skaggs puffed up with satisfaction. The other men left the room, left the two of them alone.

"Too bad Slocum didn't kill you too, Bonstall. You ain't worth a damn to me now and you gave up a chance to earn yourself five hundred easy dollars."

"Slocum could have killed me, easy, Emmett. He got the drop on me. Man's not hardly human. He don't act regular."

"What in hell you mean by that?"

"He's mighty good at leavin' no tracks, and he handles them woods like he was born there."

"He shoots pretty good, too," said Skaggs.

"He does. Hell, I wished I could have got him. Me 'n Rufus tried, God knows."

"Where'd you find him?"

"Where I figured. Out on the Crow trail, near where he kilt them others."

"You should have taken a bunch with you."

"We wanted to get him ourselfs," Bonstall said sheepishly.

"Now you're just a goddamned messenger boy for that bastard."

"I reckon Slocum means what he says."

"What's that?" roared Skaggs.

"I think he means to come after you and take this town and ever'body in it."

"The hell you say," snorted Skaggs. But Bonstall's words worried him more than he let on and when he left the saloon, he was mad as a hornet. For the first time in his life he had been beaten. And by a lone man.

John Slocum.

14

Melanie Lovelace drew a deep breath, closed the door so that Bonstall could not hear her breathing. She was almost certain he could hear the pounding of her heart. She had listened to every word of his conversation with Emmett Skaggs, and she now knew where Slocum was hiding. Somehow, she must get to him and warn him of Skaggs's plans.

She knew it would be risky trying to leave town, dangerous as anything she'd ever done before. But she couldn't let Slocum walk into town and be killed. She waited until her breathing returned to normal, until her heart stopped pounding. Bonstall was still in the saloon, lying flat on the table. She opened the door, peered out to make sure.

"Who's that?" asked Bonstall.

"Just me," she said. "Is there anything you need, Nate?"

Bonstall laughed. "If I didn't feel so bad . . ."

Melanie blushed and scurried by him, out the front door. She stood in the morning sunlight, looking up and down the street. Skaggs's men were everywhere. She looked down toward the stables. She must have a horse. She knew where the Crow trail was, had heard men speak of it ever since Pipestone had been built. Her pa had talked of it, often, as a place not to ride, ever.

She walked across the street, strode between two buildings to the back alley. Furtively, she edged along the alleyway toward the stables. The back doors were open. She slipped inside. No one was there. But Bonstall's horse and Harding's were rein-tied to stalls, still saddled. She knew the dun to be a gentle horse, and this one she led out back.

Hoisting her skirts, Melanie put a dainty foot in the stirrup, grasped the saddle horn. She pulled herself up, swung a leg over the cantle. She clucked to the horse, dug tiny heels into the dun's flanks.

She rode around the corral, headed for the timber beyond the town. A voice called out to her.

"Hey, hold up there! Where you goin', Melanie?"

She turned, saw Jethro Caudill just emerging from the stables. He carried a sawed-off shotgun in his hand.

"For a ride," she said.

"You come on back here!" Caudill shouted.

"Come on, boy," she whispered, and slapped heels to the dun's flanks. The horse started to break into a trot. She heard something behind her, saw Caudill coming toward her at a dead run. He waved the shotgun and one arm, trying to get her to stop. Melanie kept going.

"Stop, or I'll shoot," Jethro yelled.

Melanie did not look back. Then she heard the roar of the shotgun. Once, twice. She felt the spray of lead strike her in the back, in the shoulders. Pain shot through her, shock froze her. Double-ought buckshot struck the dun's rump and the horse broke into a gallop, pounded away with flying hooves in a full breakneck run.

Melanie felt the blood running down her back. She coughed, and blood spattered the back of her hand. She held onto the saddle horn as the horse continued to run eastward in the direction it had just come from. Blood oozed from small holes in its rump and its side twitched where a ball had grazed its flank.

The horse took a path through the timber. Melanie felt her bones jar and she slid from side to side on the saddle, desperately trying to keep her feet in the stirrups. The straps were too long and she could not hold her precarious footing at the speed the horse was racing. The trees sped by in a blur at the corners of her tear-filled eyes, and the pain in her back, her shoulder, did not worry her so much as the strange sound her lungs made as she tried to draw breath.

She felt as if her lungs were filled with dust, and when she blew out air, she saw the fine pink spray disintegrate like mist. Fear like none she had known before knotted her intestines, made her mind race with dread, the dread of dying, of dying alone.

Slocum heard the rabbit squeal. At first, he thought a hawk had caught its prey, but then he realized that one of his snares must have borne fruit. Quickly he raced to the game trail, to the sound of the squealing rabbit. The first snare was still unsprung, but when he came to the second, he saw the large rabbit jerking and twitching, a foot off the ground. The animal's eyes, brown and glinting with fear, widened. It struggled as Slocum drew his knife. He sliced across its throat, grasped the kicking animal until it stopped moving. He untied the loop from around its hind legs.

He gutted the rabbit, skinned it, carried it to the place

where he had set the wood for the cook fire. He struck flint and steel, showered sparks into the dry tinder. He blew on the tiny coals until the flame surged upwards, caught the squaw wood. Soon, the fire blazed, and Slocum quartered the rabbit. He skewered a chunk of fresh meat on his knife blade and held it to the fire. Flames licked the raw flesh, seared the juices inside. Slocum ate the meat when it was ready, and cooked the next piece.

He was on his third piece of rabbit, devouring it like a savage, when he heard the pound of hoofbeats. Startled, he crawled out from under the spruce tree, stood up. He drew a pistol, ran to the trail, and stood behind a tree.

He saw the dun loping toward him. Someone was hunched over the saddle. The dun slowed when it saw him, perked its ears into sharp-pointed cones. Its rubbery nostrils twitched as the horse picked up his scent.

Slocum stepped out from behind the tree. He called to the horse, grabbed the reins when it came near.

"Whoa, boy," he said.

Long hair dripped over the pommel, and Slocum's heart spasmed when he saw the blood on the saddle.

He pulled the horse to a halt.

Melanie looked down at him with tear-brimmed eyes. Slocum winced when he saw her face, saw the pain in her eyes. She seemed dazed and he knew she must be in mortal agony.

"Melanie? What happened? Somebody shoot you? You fall?"

"Shot," she groaned.

"Where? Who?"

"Back," she said, and her eyelids fluttered and she looked at him cockeyed.

She started to slide out of the saddle then and Slocum grabbed her to keep her from falling. Tenderly, he pulled her from the saddle. Blood soaked his sleeves as he turned her over on her back. Her breath sounded like wind rattling dry corn husks.

He carried her to a shady spot in a stand of spruce.

"John," she said, "don't go back."

"You shouldn't talk, Melanie."

"They're waiting for you," she gasped. "They'll kill you."

"Hush," he said, and wiped a line of cold sweat from her forehead.

He let her down easy, but she shuddered when her back touched the ground.

"I'll take a look at those wounds," he said.

"No, please. It—it hurts so much."

"Who shot you?" he asked, holding her back off the ground. He felt one of the balls of buckshot roll under the movement of his arm.

"Jethro Caudill. He—he tried to stop me."

Slocum said nothing, but his mouth tightened in a thin line. His green eyes flashed for a moment, then darkened with shadows. A kid. A damned kid. Caudill was still wet behind the ears and in the crack of his ass. Slocum had spanked him before, but now the kid had gone beyond reason, like a mad dog.

"Melanie," said Slocum softly, "I think we've got to get that lead out of your back. You're hurt bad and I don't know what I can do, but I've got to try."

"John, I'm real scared now. I feel plumb bad. I can't breathe good and I'm thinking real awful things. I mean, I guess I'm gonna die, and I don't want to. Not now. Not like this. I feel real lightheaded and I'm wondering if I go to sleep if I'll ever wake up. It's scary. I'm just scared of—of everything right now. I'm afraid for you to look at me, at my back. It hurts there, a lot. Burns. Just burns like fire, John."

"I know," he said. "Melanie, I'm real sorry."

She clutched at him and her eyes opened wide with fear. Slocum knew the look. He had seen it in the eyes of dying soldiers during the War. He had seen the same look in the eyes of men hurt on cattle drives and from bullet wounds bigger than the ones that peppered her back. He had seen the look in the eyes of game he had killed. The look in her eyes wrenched at him and tore something out of his heart and out of his belly. There was nothing he could say to her, he knew, that would comfort her. Nothing he could say or do that would stop death from falling over her like a blanket, like a heavy buffalo robe that would smother her senses, shut off her breathing forever.

He touched her back gently, felt the blood, the tiny, ragged holes where the lead pellets had punctured her flesh. She winced with pain and John winced, too, because he knew had bad it must hurt. One of the holes was high up, and it pumped a great deal of blood. He knew the ball must have punctured a lung. He heard Melanie cough and then he saw the blood and flecks of foam on her lips, the abject terror in her eyes.

She grasped his hand, squeezed it.

"John," she said, and blew pink bubbles onto her lips, "I don't want you to feel bad, too. I know I'm hurt to the quick and dying . . ."

"You're not dy—"

"Hush, John," she interrupted. "I feel real bad inside and my breath tastes like iron dust and my mouth tastes like pennies. I feel like I'm drowning, too, and it gets harder and harder to breathe." She spoke very slowly, each word forming and coming out with great effort. Slocum knew that she was probably right. She was dying and there wasn't a damned thing he could do about it.

"You've got to save your strength," he said. "I can get help. I can get you a doctor or a woman who knows medicine."

"John," she whispered, her strength fading quickly now, "there's no one in Pipestone who can doctor me and you know I'd never be able to ride to a real town. I'm so scared and yet I feel kind of at peace, too. It comes and goes. I don't know how I feel. Mad, maybe. Not at Jethro, but at myself or Fate, whatever it was that made me act so foolish. I just didn't think he would shoot."

"No," said Slocum. "You would think that." He didn't tell her what was on his mind, but if Jethro Caudill were there at that moment, he would have killed him. No questions asked.

She squeezed his hand, slumped against his lap. He pulled her close to him, held her like a child in the cradle of his arms.

He wondered that no one had followed her. He kept listening for sounds of pursuing outlaws, but the afternoon droned on, drowsy with the buzz-hum of insects, the faint whisper of breezes, and the distant caw of crows. Melanie closed her eyes and he thought she might have fainted, but he heard her whimper and they opened again, wide, and looked up into his with that god-awful fright in them that tore at his heart and made his stomach churn with anger that one so young and beautiful had to die like this, shot up like a dog with less than three ounces of brainless lead.

"John," she said, and jerked him away from his angry, tormented thoughts, "I feel real bad and lightheaded and not so much pain as my breath tasting like brass and burning in my lungs like I was breathing fire . . ."

"Just hold on, Melanie," he said, "and try to be quiet until the hurt passes."

"Is that how it is when you die? You just stop hurting and then, nothing?"

"I don't know," he said, and there was a bitter edge to his voice, a tightness that he couldn't control.

"John, I love you," she said suddenly.

Slocum said nothing, but he felt his heart pump hard as if something had squeezed it tight.

"Do you love me?" she asked.

"I reckon I do, Melanie," he said, and it wasn't much of a lie. Not now, not like this, when he knew she was dying. He loved her spirit, something about her, if not all of her. He didn't want her to die like this, didn't want her to suffer.

"I was hoping we could go—could go away someplace and get married someday, be happy, raise a family. Oh, I know you weren't thinking about all that, but I was, and I came here to warn you not to go to town because they were going to kill you. They were going to shoot you down and . . ." She broke off and began sobbing, then, and she couldn't stop. Slocum held her tightly, but the sobbing got worse and then she started coughing and then blood spilled from her lips and it was bright red, lung blood, full of oxygen and life, and then she couldn't get her breath. Her lips turned blue and her eyes got cloudy and then she rose up, struggling for breath, clawing at him like a drowning person. The blood choked her, running from the corners of her mouth, erupting like a fountain. She shuddered and her eyes blinked several times and then closed. She was death-still in his arms and Slocum knew she had gone, that she had died like that, trying hard to breathe through the blood and things torn apart inside her, the life spark snuffed for all time.

Slocum knew that although Caudill had pulled the trigger, he had acted on orders from Emmett Skaggs, and there wasn't an outlaw in Pipestone who wouldn't have done the same thing.

Melanie hadn't deserved to die like this. Someone must speak up for her, must exact vengeance on her behalf. Slocum's jaw tightened and he looked down at her waxen face, wiped the blood from her chin, and felt that squeeze of his heart again.

"Goddamn you," he breathed, "goddamn you all."

He held Melanie's lifeless body tight to his and rocked her and fought back the tears that stung his eyes.

"Yes, Melanie," he said, "I love you. Go with God, go with the wind."

He stood up, lifting her weightless body with him and stood there, his legs spread wide apart. He looked up at the sky and the rage built up in him as he thought of Emmett Skaggs and Jethro Caudill and Jack Lovelace, Melanie's worthless father, and the whole goddamned bunch of them. He wanted them to see what they had done to this young woman before he killed them, one by one, watched them go down before the wrath of his smoking guns.

He vowed, then, that they would pay, every last one of them, if not for anything else, at least for this, for the death of Melanie Lovelace.

15

Slocum washed the blood from Melanie's face and cleaned her up for the journey back to Pipestone. He could barely stand to look at her face, frozen now in death, and the smile gone forever. He knew where he had to take her, who he had to see before he started his terrible trail of vengeance on those responsible for her death. He tied her as gently and tenderly as he could to the dun horse and watched the sun go down as he rode in a slow, wide circle back to town. He wanted to get there after dark and he wanted the ride to be proper and fitting, like a funeral procession.

He skirted the rough places, sought the soft ground, guided the horse through the grasses and under tall pines that shadowed him with green boughs as the last of the light faded in the western sky. He came to the far edge of town, near where Pete Anders lived, and he waited for full dark, the dark before moonrise, before he rode for the house, leading the dun pony with its tragic burden. He had one hand on a pistol butt, as if daring someone to challenge him, so great was his rage, still.

He dismounted before he reached the house, stayed close to the black horse. He didn't want anyone to see his silhouette. Lamps burned in the house and he saw shadows behind the curtains. He ground tied the two horses, approached the house cautiously.

He came up to the back door, tapped lightly.

"Who's there?" called an anxious voice. Sally Anders, unless he missed his guess.

"Slocum," he whispered gruffly. "Open the door just a crack."

"Just a minute." He heard the sound of retreating footsteps.

Moments later, Pete Anders called out. "Slocum, that you?"

"Yes. I've got Melanie with me. Don't open the door wide."

"No, you come on in. Quick." Someone doused the lamp in the kitchen and the door creaked open. Slocum slipped inside. Anders closed and bolted the door.

"What's this about Melanie?" Pete asked, and Slocum smelled the reek of whiskey on his breath.

"She's dead. Caudill shot her."

"I know. I thought she got away."

"She lived a while," Slocum said tightly. "She's laid across that dun horse of Bonstall's out back."

"I'll help you fetch her. Want a drink first?"

"No, I don't want anything to drink."

"I understand," said Pete.

Slocum heard whispers in the kitchen, then a gasp. As he and Pete went back outside, he heard the two women sobbing. They walked to the horses. Slocum untied Mel-

anie and they lifted her down, carried her back to the
house. Sally held the door open for them. Alice led them
to her bedroom and they laid Melanie out. Alice lighted
a lamp and she and her niece hugged each other and
wept. Pete muttered a curse under his breath and left the
room.

"I cleaned her up best I could," he said, "but she could
use some care."

"We'll put a nice dress on her," said Alice, "some
powder and perfume and . . ."

She broke into sobs again and Slocum left the room. He
found Pete sitting in his favorite chair, a drink in hand. The
man looked exhausted, his eyes red-rimmed, his features
sagging in the amber glow of the lamps. Slocum sat down,
sucked in a deep breath.

"A hell of a thing," said Pete.

"Yeah," said Slocum. "Where are they?"

Pete laughed harshly. He drank from his whiskey
glass.

"They're scared, Slocum. Nobody sleeps. Everyone
lives in fear you'll come back in the night and start killing
them."

"Well, I'm here."

"Yes, you are, by gum. I hope you kill 'em all. But
they're waitin' for you, Slocum. They're waitin' and
they're mad as a swarm of spring hornets. 'Specially Jack
Lovelace."

"Lovelace?"

"He blames you for Melanie gettin' shot at. Course, he
don't know she got killed. When he finds out, there'll be
hell to pay."

"Seems to me he ought to go after Caudill."

"Jack don't figger that way. His brains is all biled and
fried from all that tanglefoot he drinks. Man's plumb loco,

and I've seen him go off like this before. He's a killer, plain and simple, but a backshooter and a rulebreaker. He don't give a man no chance, once't he's got his eye on him."

"Is Jack drinking now?" Slocum asked.

"Sober as a judge," said Pete, and slugged down the rest of his whiskey.

Emmett Skaggs looked at the men gathered in the saloon. The bar was closed, and there were no more than eight or ten men there at the moment. They would relieve some of the others who had been sitting on the rooftops, hiding behind curtained windows all afternoon. Everyone was edgy, nervous.

Except Jack Lovelace.

He sat by the door, Jack did, looking like a cat about to spring. If he'd had a tail, Emmett thought, it would be twitching. Hard to figure Jack. He was a loner, but loyal as any of his men. He professed to love his daughter, but he treated her rough when he was drunk. Still, Emmett thought he was a good father. He just went too far sometimes with the switch and the rod. Melanie was a good kid, but she shouldn't have fallen for this Slocum feller. Jack ought to whale her good when she came back. If she came back.

Emmett worried about that. Jethro said he thought he hit her with the scattergun, but Caudill was a little wild, not to be trusted a hell of a long ways from the end of his tether. Still, he, like Jack, was a good man. He wasn't afraid to shoot in a tight corner, and Emmett liked that in a young man. Reminded him of himself as a lad.

Skaggs got up from the table where he had been sitting, snuffed out his cigar. He had been inside too long. He couldn't think inside the saloon. He wanted a drink, but if he opened the bar, there would be some others who would drink, too, and he couldn't have that. Not as long as Slocum was out there, and everybody so spooked.

Damn Slocum! How could one man hold siege to a whole town? It didn't make sense. What was there about that man that had everyone buffaloed? He wasn't the law, and even if he was, he was just one man, not a posse.

Emmett walked out the back door. When Nate Wales started to follow, he waved him back.

"Gonna make the rounds," he told Wales. He wanted to be alone. He wanted to think about a lot of things. That was the hell about a siege. You had to wait. You couldn't just go out and fight. That bastard Slocum had made them all prisoners. Skaggs didn't like that.

He stepped outside, saw a man standing at the edge of the porch, a double-barreled shotgun at rest on the railing.

"Pike, that you?"

"Yeah, Emmett. Awful quiet."

"You keep listening. He could come tonight. Or before dawn."

"I seen a man like him once," said Pike, whose first name was Colin. No one called him that. They called him Corky, because he pulled cork from a bottle as good as any man and held his liquor better than most.

"Yeah?" said Skaggs, suddenly interested.

"He was a breed. Didn't have no name, but ever'body called him Shadow. Down in Tascosa, it was. He was real quiet and big and he only showed up when there was trouble. Or maybe trouble showed up when he was around. He always came out top of the heap, but then he'd go off and nobody ever saw him leave. Nobody ever knew where he went."

"So, what happened to him?"

"I don't know. He killed my partner one day and I went after him, blood in my eye. Never did pick up his trail. He just plumb disappeared."

"That doesn't make any sense, Corky."

"Nope. I always puzzled over it. I come into Soccorro, once, heard he was there, and I saw him for a minute or two. Some Mex called him out and next thing, the Mex was on the sawdust and Shadow had a smoking gun in his hand. I swear to Christ he smiled at me."

Skaggs could not hide his irritation. "Why are you telling me all this, Pike?"

"I don't know. I was thinkin' about this Slocum and Shadow and how much alike they was. I never saw Shadow after that. He got away before I could collect my few wits and I just always puzzled over it. Man comes along out of nowhere, like Shadow done, and he puts men in boot hill and then just goes off. Don't make no sense to me. He didn't make no money off his gun."

"What the hell's that supposed to mean?" Emmett demanded.

"Like Slocum. He's his own man, I reckon. Kind of chills your blood, you know what I mean."

"Pike, just tend to your business. Slocum ain't anybody."

"I know, Emmett, that's just the point. Neither was Shadow."

Skaggs stalked off the porch, his boots ringing hollow on the steps. He walked along the alley, looked up at the stars, saw the ridgeline of jagged treetops. He smelled the dark air, caught the scent of lumber still curing, the fragrant aroma of spruce and pine and fir, the dank smell of stone and earth. The moon rose as he walked, big over the ridge, big and bright and full of mystery. It would be small, once it topped the ridge, but now it was huge and ominous, so luminous he could see his shadow on the ground.

He continued his rounds, heading for the Anders place. That was the only house where he had not set a guard. He had a reason for that. He didn't trust Pete. If Slocum got any help, it would come from Pete Anders.

"Let him come," said Skaggs. "Let the bastard come."

Slocum stood up when Alice entered the front room. She looked pale, her face drawn into tight lines that made her look older than her years, yet the comeliness still there, the sturdiness of a woman visible in the set of her lips, the cant of her cheekbones.

"Melanie was hurt pretty bad," she said simply. "We saw her back, where the shot . . ."

Slocum rose from his chair, went to her. He took her in his arms, held her until the moment of overwhelming emotion passed. Sally entered the room, saw the two embracing, and blushed. She went to her father, put her arms around his shoulders.

"Did you tell Slocum about Freddie?" she asked.

"No, not yet," said Pete.

"What's that?" asked Slocum. Alice wiped her eyes, sat down on the divan, heaved a deep sigh.

"Freddie Willits come in today with supplies. More ammunition, some Henry rifles, repeaters."

Slocum hadn't seen Willits since that first time when Freddie had warned him to get out of Pipestone.

"Did you talk to him?" asked Slocum.

"Not much. He was actin' mighty strange."

"How's that?"

"Like he had somethin' in his craw. But he was kept busy unloadin' and I had all I could do to make up the inventory. Nate Wales was guardin' us, watchin' us both pretty close. Why?"

"I wondered if he had seen any men riding this way," said Slocum.

"Vigilantes?"

"The law. Citizens."

"Well, you'd have to ask him about that," said Anders. "But I got something for you."

Anders put down his glass, rose to his feet. Sally took a chair, folded her hands in her lap. Her father left the room, returned a few moments later. He was carrying a new Henry rifle, two boxes of cartridges. He handed them to Slocum.

"Snuck 'em out when I left the store," he said. "Figgered the rifle might come in handy."

Slocum grinned, took the rifle in his hands. Anders set the boxes of cartridges down on the table in front of the divan. Slocum worked the action, held the rifle to his shoulder.

"You cleaned out the grease," he said.

"Yep," said Anders.

"Thanks," said Slocum. "You took a chance, though."

"Willits did. He brought one extra. I didn't mark it down."

"I'm mighty grateful," said Slocum. He knew he owed the two men a lot. "Freddie stuck his neck out, too."

"Freddie thinks a heap of you, Slocum."

"So do we all," said Alice. "Poor Melanie. Did she . . ."

"She died peaceful," said Slocum. "You oughtn't to think about it too much."

Alice nodded, sniffled.

Slocum rubbed a sleeve across the brass receiver of the rifle, opened a box of cartridges. He fed cartridges into the magazine, levered a round in the chamber, fed another into the slot. The rifle was fully loaded. He set the hammer on half-cock. He picked up the boxes of cartridges.

"I'll be going now," he said.

"You can stay the night..." A look from her brother silenced Alice.

"No," said Slocum. "I've got to start the ball, keep Skaggs off-balance. Pete, I'll have a word with you before I go."

"I'll walk out with you."

Slocum tipped his hat to the two women. "Thanks for taking care of Melanie," he said.

"Thank you for bringing her," said Alice.

"She was in love with you," said Sally, blurting it out.

Slocum said nothing, but Alice scanned his face, her eyebrows arched, a deep questioning look in her eyes.

"Good night," said Slocum, finally. Pete followed him down the hall. They stopped in the kitchen.

"Pete, I can't wait any longer for Norman. He got away, is supposed to bring some help. I figure he might get here sometime tomorrow or the next day."

"Maybe you better hole up until then."

"No. You're in danger. So is your daughter, and your sister. Freddie Willits, too. But I want you to do something for me, for yourself."

"Name it," said Anders.

"Stay sober. You get the women out of Pipestone when you see fire and smoke. Get out of the line of fire, and stay together."

"I could help."

"Have you coal oil in the store?"

"Plenty of it," Pete replied.

"Set some cans in the stables. Hide 'em. Or as near as you can get."

"Freddie and I can handle that. You look under the tack and behind the piles of straw."

"All right. Keep your eyes peeled and be ready to get the hell out."

"I will," said Pete. "What're you going to do tonight, Slocum?"

"I'm going after Jethro Caudill first."

"You better watch out for Jack Lovelace."

"Yes. He's on my list, too."

"So long, Slocum. Good luck."

Slocum said nothing. In a minute, he was gone, swallowed up by the night. Pete heard the muffled sound of a horse's whicker, followed by hoofbeats. There were two horses moving off. He had wondered if Slocum would take the dun with him. He listened until the sounds faded.

When he went back into the house, he knew something was wrong. It was too quiet.

He walked into the front room.

Emmett Skaggs sat in Pete's chair, his pistol leveled at the women.

"Too bad I didn't get here five minutes ago, Anders," said Skaggs. "Looks like you stepped over the line."

"What are you gonna do, Emmett?" Pete asked. There was not a trace of fear in his voice.

"Why, I've already done it, son."

"How's that?"

"I just took me some hostages, Anders. Now, we'll see how far Slocum gets."

"He'll take you down, Emmett."

Skaggs looked at the two women and smiled.

Pete Anders swallowed the lump in his throat.

Now, there was fear. It looked as if Skaggs would win after all. Slocum was as good as dead.

16

Slocum rode into the fringe of timber north of town, stripped the horses of their saddles. He hobbled them, stashed the saddles in nearby brush. He might need them later, but for now, they were a liability. He emptied the cartridge boxes, stuffed shells into his pockets. He carried the rifle down to the back of a small, sod-roofed building between two larger ones.

He went between the small building and a bigger one, held up at the main street. He peered up and down the street, saw nothing. He looked at the roofs, at the vacant windows, but the darkness was too deep. Farther down, he saw pools of light in the street, from the Pinetree Lodge and the Owlhoot Saloon.

Slocum waited. Listened.

He heard a low voice down the street, then another. He strained his eyes, looking, saw a blob of shadow atop one of the false fronts as a man stood up for a minute, then ducked back down.

Slocum let out a low whistle. The man stood up again. Slocum was ready for him. He cocked the Henry, squeezed the trigger. The man screamed, clawed at his chest. Slocum didn't wait, but dashed back behind the buildings. He heard the crash as the man on the roof fell.

Then all hell broke loose, as shots sounded all along the main street. Slocum raced down the alley, hunched over, levering another shell into the Henry's chamber. He fired a round through the back window of the saloon, dashed on, sent another round crashing into the back of the hotel.

Men shot into the alley and Slocum crouched behind a low fence, waiting. The firing died down. Men shouted up and down the street, calling out names, checking shadows before firing. Slocum sat tight, invisible in the darkness, motionless when others about him were moving. If they wanted him, they would have to hunt him, but none seemed willing to do that. After a while, it grew quiet again, except for an occasional footfall or a cough, and Slocum began moving slowly along the alley, toward the western end of town.

No one challenged him and he was careful to make no sound. He saw a man pacing back and forth atop the last building on the street. When his back was turned, Slocum moved up close, rounded the building, and hugged it. Then he walked out, away from it, looking up as he did so.

Slocum's boots crunched on stone. He froze, brought his rifle up slowly to his shoulder. The man on the rooftop came to the edge, looked downward.

"Who's there?" he called.

Slocum squeezed the trigger. A cloud of white smoke spewed from the muzzle. Slocum was already running to the opposite side of the street as the man screamed and tumbled over the edge of the building to the earth below. He struck with a thud and Slocum knew he was dead before he hit the ground.

A hail of bullets flew in Slocum's direction. The bullets kicked up dust spouts at the end of the street, but Slocum had already gained the shelter of a storage shed on the opposite side of the street. He kept moving. There was nothing to be gained by staying where he was.

Angry voices called out to him.

"Come on, Slocum," they yelled. "Fight like a man!"

"Hey, Slocum, you scared to come out in the open?"

"What say, Slocum, you want to face me and my gun?"

Slocum ignored the taunts. He circled the eastern edge of the town. Someone fired a shot at a sound, but the noise was nowhere near Slocum's position. He smiled in the dark. He was getting to them. They were nervous. He halted, regained his normal breath after the run. He was somewhere near the general store, and beyond that was the livery stable. He wondered now if Pete would be able to set out the coal oil. There was always the chance that he could not. And the burning was an essential part of Slocum's plan.

He waited, weighing the details once again.

"I tell you, the man's loco," said Bonstall. "He's already killed two of us in the dark. Who's gonna be next?"

"Shut up," snarled Jack Lovelace.

"Fuck you, Jack," said Bonstall, obviously nervous, rattled. "Mackey and Harris are both dead as doornails and not a scratch on Slocum."

"Wait till daylight, Nate," said Lovelace. "I'll make wolfmeat of him."

"Shit."

Bonstall stalked off, away from any of the windows. He

looked longingly at the bar, sat down at a back corner table. He put his pistol in front of him, held it in his hand as if expecting Slocum to come charging through the bat-wing doors at any minute. Lovelace sat by the window, waiting like a cat.

Pike came in from the back porch.

"By God, I ain't stayin' out there. I never even seen Slocum come by. We ought to clear out, leave the damned town to him."

Lovelace turned around, fixed Pike with a withering look.

"You know where your horse is corraled," he told Pike.

"By God, come daylight, I just might light a shuck."

"I might go with you," said Bonstall, apparently glad to have an ally. "If we live long enough."

"What's the matter, Pike," sneered Lovelace, "you scared of Slocum, too?"

"No, I'm not afraid of any man I can see. But Slocum's just picking us off like turkeys, one by one. No good sense in that."

"You're lily-livered, just like Bonstall there," said Lovelace, and turned back to the window. Pike started to say something, but held back. The other men in the room began muttering among themselves, though, and Bonstall began to get nervous again. Pike turned away from him, sat at the bar, alone. He looked calm enough and Nate was sure that he wasn't a coward, but they were all facing a man who held all the cards. Slocum knew exactly where they were. They didn't have the least idea where he was at any given moment. It was terrifying to Bonstall. He wiped sweat off his forehead, rubbed his palms on his trouser legs. His lips quivered uncontrollably and he looked as if he was about to bolt from the room. The other men sensed his fear and avoided looking at him for more than a fleeting moment. Bonstall felt the hostility and he began to murmur something under his breath, something no one in the room could hear. His voice gradually grew louder until it was like a high-pitched whine.

With a shout, Bonstall leaped from the table. Pistol in hand, he dashed through the batwing doors and out into the night.

He ran down the dark street, screaming Slocum's name.

"Slocum! Slocum!"

The men on the rooftops looked down at him. Curtains moved as other men looked out at Bonstall, who was brandishing his gun and calling out to the enemy. The outlaws shook their heads. Jethro Caudill laughed insanely as Bonstall ran past.

"Crazy bastard," he said aloud.

"Slocum! Slocum! I'm coming, Slocum!"

Slocum heard the shouts. It took him a moment to realize that someone was screaming his name. Not just shouting it, but screaming it. And the voice was coming closer. Was it a trick?

Slocum hugged the building at the end of the street. Now he recognized Bonstall's voice. He peered around the corner of the building, saw the man running toward him, a pistol raised overhead.

Slocum brought his rifle up, steadied it against the side of the building. Closer and closer Bonstall came and Slocum set the sights on him, lined them up. He let Bonstall come on, then he slowly squeezed the trigger. The rifle boomed and slammed against his shoulder. Flame and smoke belched from the muzzle. At two hundred yards, Bonstall walked right into the .44-40 projectile.

Slocum saw Bonstall go down as if tripped. The pistol flew out of his hand and Bonstall pitched forward, skidded several feet before he stopped. He writhed there for a few moments, but no one came to help him. He kicked his legs, but he did not get up. After a few more moments, he lay completely still. Someone cursed.

Then men began shooting down toward the end of the street. Splinters flew off the building where Slocum had stood. A glass shattered.

Then it was quiet.

Emmitt Skaggs was annoyed that Pike was not at his post. He herded Anders, Sally, and Alice through the back door of the saloon. At that moment, Bonstall raced out the front and there was confusion until the single shot rang out.

"Pike," said Skaggs. "Keep a gun on these people."

The shooting started after that, and Skaggs looked outside in disgust.

"What in hell are they shooting at?" he asked.

"Shadows," said Pike, but he didn't smile.

Skaggs waited in the saloon until dawn. Others came and went, reported in, but no one had seen anything. The Anders family sat at a table, watched by Pike, then others who came and went. It was unnerving, just sitting there, waiting for something to happen. Finally, just a few minutes after dawn, they heard someone shout. Skaggs rose from his chair, knocked it over. Lovelace went to the window, stood there.

"There he is!" shouted Jethro Caudill. "I seen Slocum."

Skaggs stood next to Lovelace and looked out onto the street. Caudill stood there, pointing. Men on the rooftops looked down the street, too.

"I don't see nothin'," one of them said.

"He was right there," screeched Caudill, seemingly on the verge of hysteria. "I saw him."

"Bullshit," said the man on the roof just across the street.

Seconds later, Caudill went into a crouch. He dropped his sawed-off shotgun. He drew his pistol. Skaggs thought he looked very fast. Right up to the moment when another pistol exploded with a sharp crack and Jethro Caudill skidded backward two feet, propelled by a slug that caught him high in the chest. There was another explosion and Caudill danced sideways, spun in a tight circle, then dropped. The man on the roof across the street lifted his rifle, took aim. Before he fired, another explosion sounded, and he slumped over the false front. His rifle clattered as it struck the small roof and slid down to the edge, fell into the street.

"Christ," muttered Skaggs.

"Lovelace!" called out a voice.

"That's Slocum," said Pike.

"Shut up, Corky," said Lovelace. "He's callin' me."

"Well, answer him," said Skaggs impatiently.

"Yeah, Slocum! I hear ya!" yelled Lovelace. His voice echoed in the saloon. Pike licked dry lips. Skaggs backed away from the window, drew his pistol.

"I'm callin' you out, Lovelace," yelled Slocum.

"Wait," said Skaggs. "Let's get some men in position. This is our chance to get Slocum."

Lovelace turned away from the window, looked at Skaggs.

"No," he said, "this is my fight. Let me get it over with. I'll get him or he'll get me."

"Don't be stupid, Jack," said Skaggs. "Look what happened to Caudill there, and Bernie MacDonald on the roof."

"Leave me be," said Lovelace stubbornly.

"Fair fight, Slocum?" he called out through the window

and the pane shook with the force of his voice.

"Fair fight," shouted Slocum. They all heard him, but no one could see him.

"Where is he?" asked Skaggs.

"I don't know," said Lovelace, "but I'm going out there. If he cheats, he's all yours."

Skaggs tried to restrain Lovelace, but Jack shook off the man's hand and strode through the batwing doors of the saloon. He walked out to the center of the street, looked both ways.

"I don't see you, Slocum," Lovelace yelled.

"I'm over here," said Slocum. He stepped out of the livery stable. No one but Lovelace could see him from that angle. Slocum knew there was no one behind him or above him who could get off a shot. He had picked his place carefully.

The back door was open, so he could make his escape. He had emptied the coal-oil lamps in the stable, spread the oil over the straw and hay, mixed in some black powder. He was ready.

"I see you, Slocum," said Lovelace. It was very quiet as men pressed against the saloon window, strained to see down the street. But, like with Caudill, they could only see Lovelace.

"Start counting," said Slocum.

His hand hovered over the butt of his Colt. The rifle leaned against the inside wall of the stable, three feet away. The other Colt was tucked in his belt behind his back.

"To three," said Lovelace.

"Fine," said Slocum. "Get to it."

"One . . . two . . ." At the count of three, Lovelace drew his pistol. The saloon window was crowded with faces looking out. Lovelace was faster than Caudill. He was very fast. Everyone in the saloon who was looking out saw that.

They saw the slow smile break on Jack's face and they thought he would win, after all.

But Slocum's hand was a blur of speed as he jerked his pistol from its holster, cocked it on the rise, and squeezed the trigger. Lovelace fired a shot into the ground as he was blown backwards against the steps leading to the saloon, a bullet in the center of his forehead.

No one spoke for several seconds.

Then Skaggs bellowed, "Get him!"

Men came boiling out of the saloon. Slocum ducked back inside the livery stables. Pistols barked. Rifles boomed. Bullets flew in all directions, peppered the walls of the stables, tore out chunks of woods, chewed out splinters. Slocum picked up the Henry and started shooting men, knocking them down. Pike took a bullet in his gut. Slocum shot another man in the leg. The outlaws began to scramble for cover, but some of them charged him.

Slocum turned, raced through the livery stable. He struck a sulphur match, dropped it in a pool of coal oil and black powder. The black powder ignited with a *whoosh* and the oil caught fire. The straw burst into flames. The gunpowder set off more fires and the outlaws pouring into the stables were driven back by a wall of flames.

A column of black smoke rose in the sky as Slocum raced out the back.

He heard a whoop and then saw them ride out of the hills, dozens of men, Norman in the lead. He heard the thunder of their hooves. He saw them divide and then swarm into Pipestone. The outlaws, horseless, began shooting, scrambling in all directions. Norman and his men showed no mercy, shot them down.

Slocum raced between the livery and the general store, stormed into the saloon.

Skaggs had Sally around the throat, a pistol to her temple.

"I'll kill her unless you drop that rifle," said Skaggs.

Slocum, in a half-crouch, the rifle thrust forward, froze.

"Kill her, then," said Slocum evenly. "But that'll be the last thing you ever do in this life."

Skaggs thought about it. He saw Slocum's finger tightening on the trigger of the Henry.

In a rage, Skaggs hurled Sally to the floor, turned his pistol on Slocum. He squeezed the trigger. Slocum fired at the same instant. The bullet caught Skaggs square in the gut. Skaggs's bullet whistled past Slocum's ear.

Skaggs went to his knees. Slocum worked the lever quickly, squeezed the trigger again. The hammer fell with a click. Empty. Skaggs raised his pistol, took deadly aim. Slocum let the rifle fall from his hands, but he knew he was too late. He would never draw his pistol in time.

A shot rang out and Skaggs's head exploded. He pitched forward. Behind Slocum, Freddie Willits cackled. He waved a smoking pistol above his head.

"Whooee!" he shouted. "Them outlaws are going down like wheat under a scythe. I surely wanted to do my part. Looks like Emmett got the drop on you, Slocum."

"Looks like," said Slocum.

"Would you really have let him shoot me?" asked Sally.

"No, but if I had let him think that I cared, he would have killed us both."

"I know that now. He was an evil man. I'm glad you killed him."

Slocum put his arms around her. Pete slapped him on the back. Alice hugged him.

Norman came into the saloon. "We got 'em, Slocum, thanks to you."

"All of 'em?"

"Every last one. And the boys are setting a torch to the town."

"We've got a burial to do, Pete," said Slocum, "and you better pack your things, you and the women. There won't be anything left of Pipestone after today. Nothing but ashes."

"Good riddance," said Pete. "Freddie, can you help us pack and bury poor Melanie Lovelace?"

"Shore can."

"Well, Slocum," said Norman, "I'll be seeing you. Thanks again."

"Thank you, Lou," said Slocum. Both men grinned. Slocum picked up the Henry, gave it back to Freddie. Freddie smiled.

Slocum put his arms around the two women, led them out of the saloon. They walked down the main street, past the bodies of the dead outlaws.

And the ugly town of Pipestone burned like the fires of hell as they walked away toward freedom.

431